Double-Barrel Horror
Volume 2

John Boden, Simon Dewar, Patrick Freivald, Chad Lutzke, Karen Runge and M.B. Vujacic

edited by Matthew Weber

Double-Barrel Horror *is a collection of fictional horror stories. The tales presented here are intended to disturb. They are likely to include death, graphic violence, profanity, sexual content, and other themes and images that commonly disturb. If you can't deal with these themes in your fiction, then you should avoid this book.*

Copyright © 2017 Pint Bottle Press, John Boden, Simon Dewar,
Patrick Freivald, Chad Lutzke, Karen Runge and M.B. Vujacic

cover art by Brian Burks

www.pintbottlepress.com

ISBN-13: 978-1-945005-87-9

ISBN-10: 1-945005-87-4

Contents

Pint Bottle Press
99¢
DOUBLE-BARREL HORROR
BLINKY
THE MIDNIGHT SHOW
M.B. VUJACIC

Blinky

by M.B. Vujacic

"Look at this guy. Just look at him."

Emily glanced up from her phone. Her gaze shifted from a woman on the sidewalk, to the cars waiting at the traffic light up ahead, to the big red Jeep trundling down the opposite lane. Gray, featureless sky. Rain inbound. She sighed and shifted in her seat, careful not to ruffle her dress.

"God, he's pissing me off," Rod said, tensing his fists on the steering wheel.

"Who? The Jeep?"

"No. The guy behind us."

She looked over her shoulder. A white car tailed them, so close she couldn't see its headlights. Its paint was old and chipped and spattered with bird droppings, the corner of its greasy windshield sporting a crack barely held in check with a duct tape X. Its balding, bespectacled driver was leaning forward in his seat like a child peeking over the steering wheel.

"These damn people," Rod said, shaking his head. "Why would anyone drive like this? A dog could run into the street and I'd have to brake, and then we'd all be sorry. And for what? Is he gonna get somewhere faster because he's driving right up people's asses? Don't they teach them about personal space? Jesus Christ."

They reached the traffic light and stopped behind a pair of leather-clad bikers. The white car stopped behind them. The driver swung the door and stepped out. He really was short. Five foot three, if that. Sixty-something. A belly like a badly concealed basketball stretching the front of his polo shirt. Ill-fitting beige pants with baggy hips and cuffs crumpled on top of dirty running shoes. Wrinkled face set around a sharp little nose. Thin lips forming an inverted U.

He tapped his knuckles on Rod's window. Rod looked at him through the glass, his hands tightening on the wheel, and said, "What the hell do you want?"

"Don't be like that, Rod," Emily said. "Maybe he needs our help with something."

The man knocked again and made a cranking gesture with his hand, his murky gray eyes fixed on Rod. Rod licked his lips, then lowered the window. "What is this?"

"I seen some blinkies in my time," the man said, "but gosh darn it, you take the cake."

"Huh?"

"You don't know what a blinky is?"

"What the fuck are you talking about?"

The man flinched at the F word as if stung. "A blinky," he said, emphasizing each syllable as if educating a toddler, "is an inconsiderate brat who leaves his frigging blinker on while driving. Like that." He jabbed his finger at the dashboard, where the left-hand turn indicator was blinking on and off. Emily tried to recall the last time they'd taken a turn. It had been some minutes.

"Do you realize how pesky that is to other motorists?" the man said. "We keep expecting you to go left. But no, every time we think you're finally going to leave the frigging lane, you just keep going straight. And what about pedestrians who have to wait before they cross because they think you're going to—"

"Oh fuck you," Rod said. "At least I don't drive right up people's asses. Learn to keep your fucking distance in traffic. Jesus Christ."

Emily tugged at his shoulder. "Rod, let's go. The light is green."

The man gasped. "You foulmouthed brat."

"Fuck off, you crazy shit, you're the fucking blinky," Rod said. With that, he stepped on the gas and followed the other cars across the intersection. He waited for Blinky to recede into the distance before switching off the turn signal. "Can you believe that? Goddamn freak."

"You shouldn't have been so mean."

"Drives up people's asses and then gives them crap for forgetting a blinker. What a loon."

Emily sighed. Rod kept ranting, so she tuned him out and leaned back to watch the scenery. Gray suburban buildings. An orange kiosk next to a bus station. A corner drugstore with racks of fresh vegetables by the entrance. An ice cream-toting brunette winking at them from a billboard.

"Well, I'll be..." Rod said, staring at the rearview mirror. Sure enough, the ugly white car was back. Catching up fast. The sight of it brought an icy twist to Emily's stomach. Blinky must really be giving it to the gas pedal.

The traffic light ahead shone red. Rod slowed to a halt. Blinky stopped behind them, threw the door open, and marched to their car. His cheeks had turned scarlet, and a thick vein stood out on his forehead like a mountain range on a 3D map. Rod leaned out and said, "Stop harassing us or I'm gonna call the cops. I'm serious."

"You foulmouthed brat. You apologize for what you said. You apologize right this instant!"

"What? I'm not apologizing for shit."

"You said I'm crazy. You called me a crazy sh-sh-sh..." He took a deep breath and drew his fingers through his meager hair. "You apologize right now."

"Fuck you, Blinky."

Blinky gasped. "Frig me? *Frig me*?! Frig *you*, you frigging brat!"

His hand flew behind his back and returned with a large chrome sidearm and pointed it at Rod's face. Emily opened her mouth to scream. A bang like a hand clap. Wet chunks splattering over the radio, the dashboard, the steering wheel. Rod's body jerked once and slumped over the window frame, the back of his head gaping like a deformed mouth. Emily shrieked.

"Stop that noise!" Blinky shouted, his voice high-pitched like a child's. He slapped his fists against his ears. "Stop it! I'm sick and tired of all you brats always yelling and screeching at people! I can't stand it anymore! All my life I had to put up with—"

"Help!" Emily screamed, fumbling at her seat belt. "Somebody!"

"I said quiet!" He swung the pistol toward her just as her thumb found the clasp button. She yanked at the door handle and shoved against it. She heard a bang and a buzz like a bee flying past her ear, and then her elbow met the asphalt. Gasping, she pulled her legs out of the car and scrambled across the road on all fours.

Another gunshot. A plume of dust burst from the ground a foot from her. Emily leaped to her feet and broke into a run. A few lopsided steps later, she realized she had lost one of her high heels. She kicked the other one off and dashed for the sidewalk.

"No! Don't you run, woman! Come back this instant! You can't do this to me!"

Emily rushed past the traffic light and sprinted over the intersection. She looked back to see him maybe a dozen yards behind her, arms pumping, his red face a wrathful mask. He raised the pistol and she screamed and ducked her head, throwing her hands up as if that would make a difference. The bullet chipped the wall above her scalp. She saw a bus station and ran toward it.

"You won't escape!" he screamed. "I know you brats! You always get away with making trouble! But you're gonna pay this time! You're gonna pay!"

"Help!" she screamed.

An elderly couple and a trio of boys waited at the station. They looked at Emily and Blinky. "That guy is packing," a lanky boy said, and all three of them spun on their heels and raced down the sidewalk. The elderly gent moved to stand between the old lady and the incoming Emily. He wore a checkered shirt and a blazer, and his pants were pulled up over his belly button. He extended an arm toward Emily, though whether to offer aid or shield himself, she couldn't tell.

"Don't you involve them in this!" Blinky yelled. "Stop right there!"

The gun barked, and the glass wall of the bus station exploded. It barked again, and the old man's neck bloomed. Another shot, and he lurched as if punched in the chest and stumbled against Emily. She lost her balance and went down on one knee. Her dress tore down the side with a loud *rip*.

Blinky and the old lady shrieked simultaneously. The old lady took a wobbling step. Then her hand went to a spot below her collarbone where blood was spreading over white satin like a red inkblot. She collapsed with a soft thud.

"No! No, no, no! Look what you did! Look what you brats made me do!"

Emily regained her feet and kept running. Blinky let out an incoherent howl and resumed the chase. He was overweight and decades her senior, but she was barefoot and out of shape and he was closing the distance, his legs pumping in mad rhythm. Drivers who saw them turned their cars and sped away. Two girls across the street spotted the gun in Blinky's hand and backed against a nearby building like chameleons trying to meld with the scenery. The taller one raised a phone and started recording.

Then, salvation. A police cruiser, parked next to a coffee shop. A silver-haired officer in the driver's seat, reading a newspaper. She screamed, "Help!" just as another officer emerged from the coffee shop. In his hands, a cup carrier with two large cappuccinos.

The second cop looked at her and Blinky. His eyes widened. The cup carrier fell from his hand as he reached for his pistol, the cappuccinos erupting all over the sidewalk in a brown spray. *Bang, bang, bang.* Something bit Emily's calf and she went down, skinning her arms and knees. She grabbed at her leg and her hand came back wet and crimson. She moaned and looked to the cop for help, but he was no longer there. He'd fallen against the wall of the coffee shop and sunk to the ground to sit in the cappuccino puddle. Red pumped from a hole in his neck.

In the cruiser, the silver-haired cop dropped the mic and opened his door and rested his pistol on the roof and fired. Blinky fired back. Bullet holes crisscrossed the car's door, and the cop grunted and toppled behind the car and out of sight.

"No, I won't drop it!" Blinky screamed in reply to a demand that had never been made. "You can't make me! I don't answer to you! You're done making me do things! My fate is my own now!"

Slowly, leaning on her arms, Emily put her feet under her and tried to prop herself up, but her injured leg flared, her knee buckled, and she fell with a cry. A pale shadow touched her. She looked up to see Blinky pointing the gun at her. "I told you. I told you you were gonna pay. All my life I watched you brats get away with everything. But no more. No more! I won't let you do me like that anymore. From now on, justice will be served."

"Please-"

He pulled the trigger.

Click.

He looked at the gun as if it was an alien artifact. His nose crinkled and his mouth pulled down like he'd swallowed something spoiled. "Gosh darn it," he said. "Gosh darn it to heck!" Then he reached into his back pocket and drew out a fresh magazine.

Quickly, keeping her injured leg in the air, she scuttled to the coffee shop and grabbed the door handle. Holding on to it, she pulled herself up and hopped into the shop on one foot. A cheap establishment with a busted ceiling fan and scratched metal tables and chairs not meant to be sat in for long. Half a dozen people inside. A couple ducked under their table. An obese woman dropped her donuts and trundled into the toilet and locked the door. A waiter threw a chair through a back window before trying to dive outside, only to misjudge his leap and shred his arms on the glass. A teenager held his phone against his ear in a trembling hand. A young mother stood by the counter with a little boy. The kid was holding a muffin, his mouth brown with chocolate.

"Police," Emily said, the word a squeak. "Call the police!" She hopped inside. Past the bleeding waiter and the cowering couple and the young mother with her boy. She ducked under the bar flap and hid behind the counter.

"Where is she?!" Blinky screamed, kicking in the door. Everyone else screamed too. "You're hiding her from me!

Don't you dare hide her! You're all the same! All you brats are of the same cloth!"

Another gunshot. Deafening in the small shop. It stabbed Emily's eardrums like a hot needle, replacing most noises with ringing and rendering the rest distant and vague. Muffled screams. She peeked around the counter to see the teenager lying curled on his side like a dying rodent. The waiter tried to crawl under a table. Blinky saw him and shouted soundlessly at him and the waiter raised a bloody hand to protect his face. Blinky put a bullet through palm and skull both.

"Where is she?! I won't let this injustice stand! I won't! Where the frig is she?!"

The young mother turned to the counter and, for a split second, her blue eyes met Emily's. Her features were young, freckled, barely out of high school. And full of determination.

Emily opened her mouth to shriek. To tell her to stop. To drop on her knees and beg for mercy. But the girl pushed her kid behind her and grabbed a mug from the counter and flung it like a baseball. It broke against Blinky's face. He let out an "Ow!" and reeled, slapping bits of porcelain from his eyes. The girl charged him, raising her fists like an action star.

Bang, bang, bang, bang. Red spots opened in the girl's back. She stumbled and fell and lay still. Blinky said, "Gosh darn you," and shot her two more times.

Emily hid behind the counter again. The boy lay stunned a couple feet from her, looking around as if unaware how he'd come to be here, his chocolate-stained mouth gaping to reveal gums still sprouting baby teeth. She pulled him to herself and hugged him. "I'm sorry, honey," she muttered into his hair. "I'm so sorry."

Then Blinky was there, the barrel of his gun staring at her like an empty eye socket. His glasses were gone, his face a web of lacerations. "Gotcha. Told you you can't run. All my life I've been done in by your kind, but no more. Enough is enough, I say."

"Please," Emily whimpered, turning to shield the boy with her body. "Please, don't hurt the child."

Gunshots crack like thunder.

***

A white car passed outside and Emily drew in a hissing breath.

It wasn't Blinky's car. Not even close. This one was bigger, newer, freshly washed. Still, she stared at it wide-eyed until it passed, her coffee cup hovering an inch from her mouth, her pulse hammering in her temples. Somewhere close, a fly buzzed.

"Miss? Are you all right?"

Emily swallowed. She lowered her cup without taking a sip. The hands clutching it were thin and pale, the skin around the fingernails gnawed raw. The sun and the warmth outside clashed with her black shirt, black pants, heel-less black shoes. Her hair was tied in a tight bun. No jewelry. Resting against her chair, a brown cane still glossy from the store.

The man sitting across the table from her turned to look through the coffee shop window at the street outside. His face was all sharp angles and piercings polished to a shine, one on his brow, another above his chin. He sported a slim goatee, and his dyed blond hair was beginning to recede. The journalist identification dangling around his neck named him A. LEE. "Did you see something?"

Emily dropped her gaze. "No, I... I mean, there was a white car. For a moment, I..."

Lee gave a solemn nod, then took his tablet and added a few more lines to the wall of text he had written during their conversation. She had expected him to record the interview with the same device, but he used a silvery dictaphone. She didn't ask why. In the weeks following what the newspapers had dubbed the *Coffee Shop Horror*, she had declined too many interviews to count, wishing only to grieve in peace. Then the bill for Rod's funeral arrived and she found herself in desperate need of extra funds. So there she was, back in that nameless coffee shop with the dead ceiling fan—Lee thought revisiting the location of the massacre would make the interview more "genuine"—talking about the worst day of her life to the highest bidder.

"What is your opinion of Officer Norton?"

"He... He saved my life. He even sent me a get-well card while I was in the hospital. I think the world of him."

Norton was the silver-haired cop who had been sitting in the cruiser when she came running to the coffee shop. Blinky shot him in the arm. The bullet chipped an artery. Norton applied a tourniquet, stumbled into the shop, and ended Blinky with a triple tap to the back. His photo came out in the papers with HERO COP printed under it in big blocky letters.

Later, after she had answered all of Lee's questions and he was reaching for the dictaphone, she grabbed his hand and said, "Wait, I... I would like to add something."

"Of course. Please do."

"This, uh... This all happened because... Because my brother was rude to that man. I mean, I know the man was insane and that it probably would've made no difference, but..."

"Go on."

"People should be nicer to each other. Even if it's some stranger, you never know what goes on in their head, or if they have a knife or a gun... You just never know."

Lee watched her as if expecting her to say more. When she didn't, he nodded and said, "Thank you."

"I thought you'd ask me if I knew the man's name."

"I know you don't."

"You do?"

He shut off his tablet and his dictaphone. "Yep. I have my sources. I know the police don't have a clue."

"They didn't find anything?"

"Nope. The guy carried no ID, and his face wasn't in any database. His picture has been in the papers for days now, and no family or friends have come in with any information. They know he was about sixty and that, for the past eight years, he'd worked at a gas station out in the desert. Double shifts. His boss knew him only as Walter. Paid him in cash. Said he was a little on the strange side."

Her mouth twisted.

He pushed his tongue against the inside of his cheek, as if considering something. Then he leaned closer and said, "Probably shouldn't tell you this, but people have reported sightings."

"Sightings?"

"Yeah. Of Walter, or whatever his real name is."

"But... He died. I saw it."

"I know, but after his pictures came out in the news, people have called the police saying they've seen someone who looks like him. Normally, the cops ignore these things, but there's been lots of these sightings. Most were near a shooting range a few miles from the gas station where Walter worked. Almost as if—"

The top of Lee's head exploded. Warm stickiness splashed over Emily's face and then she heard screams. From herself, the waitress, the patrons. Through a crimson mist, she saw a short man in the doorway. Blinky. His hair was grayer, his spectacles were thicker, and the belly disfiguring his shirt was rounder, but Blinky nonetheless. A magazine belt around his waist. Smoking in his hands, an assault rifle.

"Which one of you foul-minded brats is the skunk who got my little brother shot?!" he roared, spraying spittle. "Gosh darn it, there'll be heck to pay!"

With that, he squeezed the trigger.

The Midnight Show

by M.B. Vujacic

The show sucked.

Worse, it wasn't going to get better. Will realized this halfway through the second performance—a sorry juggling act featuring a couple who looked too old for their gaudy costumes and whose juggling clubs resembled worn bowling pins. He wished he could enjoy the clowns and the lion tamer as much as his little sister did. But Amanda was six, and he was thirteen. Unlike her, he was old enough to understand that first impressions mattered, and that if a show opened with a whimper, it was unlikely to go out with a bang.

It was his fault, really. He should've known. The day the circus came to town, he and Clyde and a bunch of other kids had gathered to watch it set up shop. They'd arched their brows at the patchy tent and laughed at the dilapidated trucks decorated with crappy drawings of clowns and elephants and trapeze artists. Even the posters looked like they'd been salvaged from an 80s time capsule. Everything about the *Saint Armenides Circus* screamed cheap. And lame. And worst of all, boring. Yet when his parents suggested they go on a little family outing and check it out, Will's curiosity got the better of him and he said, "Sure, how bad could it be?"

According to the internet, traveling circuses were a dying breed. Watching the "lion tamer" lead out half a dozen Great Danes clad in canine versions of ballet dresses, only to make them "dance" to some girly song, Will thought maybe this decline was a good thing. Aside from the smallest kids, the audience appeared either half-asleep or more interested in their phones.

Will sighed. If only Clyde was seated next to him, they could joke about the terrible show. But Clyde and his parents had arrived late and ended up getting the rearmost seats, a good three rows behind Will. He looked over his shoulder, scanning the crowd in search of Clyde's round face. He found him sitting between his bear of a father, and a tall girl with chestnut hair that spilled down her cheeks and neck and arms and seemingly continued to the small of her back. Her hand rested on Clyde's shoulder. She was whispering in his ear. Clyde smiled and nodded, wriggling his meaty hands.

Will had never seen her before. He'd also never seen Clyde chat with a girl, let alone one this pretty. Like a total jerk, he felt a pang of jealousy. He kept stealing peeks at the pair. They were engrossed in conversation, her hand caressing Clyde's shoulder or stroking his hair.

"Willie," Amanda said, tugging at his sleeve.

"Don't call me that. It's either Will or William or—"

"Why is the clown sad?"

"Huh?"

"Why is the clown sad?" Amanda repeated, thrusting her index finger at the arena, where a clown had accidentally sawed off his own hand and was trying to reattach it with superglue. He wore a scarlet wig and a crimson jumpsuit adorned with bells and technicolor ribbons. His face and neck were slathered white, with large red smears around his lips that made his mouth look puckered. His eyes looked like they were weeping blood.

"I'd be sad too, if I was working in the world's crappiest circus," Will said, though to him the clown didn't seem sad at all. Mean or demented, but not sad.

It was the last act of the evening, thank God. Will hurried ahead of Amanda and their parents, slipping past yawning people who shuffled from their seats like toilers heading home after a day of mindless grind. He found Clyde and the girl outside. Clyde's mom and dad stood nearby, smoking. Orange sunset sky. Long shadows. A head taller than Clyde and Will and a year or two their senior, the girl really did grow her hair well to her hips. She giggled at something Clyde said, and Will felt the sting of jealousy all over again. Then Clyde waved, and Will sucked in his belly and threw back his shoulders and approached them.

"Hey, Will," Clyde said. "Sombra, this is my best friend Will. Will, this is Sombra."

"What sorta name is Sombra?" Will said, trying to sound like the high school kids he sometimes saw smoking cigarettes in the park.

She laughed. "It's Spanish."

"You don't look Spanish."

She laughed again. "Is Will your real name?"

"No, it's William."

"I knew it. I bet people call you Willy. With a Y."

Clyde tittered.

Will forced a chuckle. In his cheeks, a furnace. "Yeah, no. Anyway, I, uh, I haven't seen you before. You new to town?"

"Just passing through. I'm with the circus."

"You work there?"

"Nah, my dad just lets me tag along. He's the clown."

"Oh."

"You liked his act?"

"Yeah, I loved it," Clyde said.

"It was okay," Will said.

Sombra let out a high-pitched laugh that made Will's eardrums itch. "You two are so full of shit."

Will and Clyde exchanged a look.

"My dad's act sucks," she went on. "And don't look at me like that. He knows it too. Everybody knows it. All of their acts suck."

"Why do them, then?" Will asked.

Sombra tilted her head like an inquisitive canine and grinned. Only it wasn't just any grin. Her lips stretched almost to her cheekbones, forming a fleshy triangle filled with pearly teeth and red gums. And she stared at them. And stared. And stared. Will shifted his weight from foot to foot, unable to meet her gaze. "I'm gonna let you in on a secret," she said.

Will licked his lips. "Umm, okay?"

"The show you watched. The circus act. It's not the real one."

"What do you mean?" Clyde said.

She leaned in closer, conspiratorial, and spoke quietly, "There is another show. *That* one is the real deal. But it's not for kids."

"You mean, like, strippers?" Will asked.

"Better than that. It's hardcore stuff."

"What kinda stuff?"

"Special orders. Customized performances. Audience members go to some websites and vote on what they wanna see, and my dad and the others make it happen. We call it the Midnight Show."

Will frowned. "That's a load of crap."

"Wanna bet?"

"Sure. Twenty?"

"Fifty," Sombra said, and held out her hand. Will's frown deepened. He stared at that hand, tracing the thin scars curving across the palm and the fingers. "What, you don't have fifty bucks?" she said, her hand hovering in midair.

"I'm thirteen. Of course I don't have fifty bucks."

She rolled her eyes. "Let's do your twenty then. C'mon."

"How will I know you're not lying?"

"Cause I'll take you to the Midnight Show so you can see for yourself."

"But you said it's not for ... not for minors."

"I'll sneak us in. I do it all the time."

"You coming, boy?" Clyde's giant of a father called from a car so small, he looked like a turtle poking its head out of its shell.

"Uh, right away, dad," Clyde said, and turned to Sombra. "I wanna go. I wanna see the Midnight Show."

"Boy!"

"You will," Sombra said, her hand still hanging between Will and her like an ultimatum. "I'll see you tonight."

Clyde climbed into the little car, and it drove off trailing blue exhaust.

"C'mon Willy with a Y," Sombra said. "Make up your mind. Hand's getting tired."

Will shook his head.

Her arm dropped to her side. "Chicken."

His mouth twisted. "Whatever. What do you want from Clyde?"

"What kinda question is that?"

"Girls don't normally talk to him. Especially not older ones."

"I'm no regular girl. Besides, I wanna meet cool new people in the towns I visit."

Will furrowed his brows. Clyde? Cool? Clyde was the class nerd. Half the kids called him Fatso. Or Tits. He was Will's best friend and Will loved him like a brother, but by no means was he cool.

"Anyway, I gotta go," Sombra said. "Gotta help my dad fix his makeup."

"What for? The show is done for today."

She giggled. "No, Will-y. The show has yet to begin."

With that, she strode off and went into one of the circus trucks, the ends of her hair twirling over the top of her skirt. Someone tapped his shoulder, and he realized Amanda and their parents were standing behind him, his mom asking the name of his new lady friend. By then, the sun had sunk from sight and a pale blue twilight had taken over.

"She's not my friend," he said, and headed to the car.

***

His phone vibrated with a sound like a robot farting.

Will looked up from the comic book in his hands. The phone vibrated again. He sat in his bed and picked the phone up by the cable and unplugged it from its charger. On the screen, Clyde's ruddy face. Will tapped the green *Answer* icon. "Whaddup, dude?"

"Dude, come to the window," Clyde said.

"To the window? My window?"

"No, Donald Trump's."

Will snorted and kicked off the thin covers emblazoned with various superheroes. He went to the window and leaned outside and there they were, Clyde and Sombra, two murky figures on the sidewalk, their backs to the streetlamp. Sombra's hair framed her face like a hood, shrouding her features in darkness. Clyde waved.

"What are you doing here?" Will hissed into the phone.

"Come with us, dude."

"You crazy? Come with you where?"

"To the Midnight Show."

"It's *past* midnight, Clyde. Jesus Christ."

"Come on, dude." Then, quietly, as if afraid Sombra would hear. "They got strippers."

"Jesus Christ," Will said again.

"Seriously, man. When's the next time we're gonna get a chance to see strippers?"

"Forget it. Go home."

"Please, man. I really wanna go."

"No."

"What are you afraid of?"

"I'm not afraid."

"Then come with us."

"Go home, Clyde."

"Come on, dude. I know you wanna see them."

Will bit his lip. "Wait there," he whispered. He opened his door and peeked into the hallway, ready to tell whoever he saw that he was going to the toilet. The hallway was empty. He tiptoed to his parents' bedroom and pressed his ear to the door. Snoring.

This is insane, Will thought as he returned to his room. He distrusted Sombra and didn't want to leave Clyde alone with her. He couldn't rat him out to his parents, either. Clyde would never forgive him. Damn.

Will put on a pair of jeans and a baseball shirt and headed out, sweat glistening on his forehead. A warm, windless evening. A dead black sky. A hush in the street. Two figures watching him from the sidewalk—one squat and rotund, the other tall and wiry. He kept looking back at his house. In the windows, darkness.

Sombra turned and strode down the street, her hair flowing behind her like a veil. Clyde beckoned to Will, then hurried after her. Will pulled the yard door open, cringing at the squealing hinges. He caught up with Clyde and grabbed his shoulder and whispered, "Why didn't you tell me you were gonna do this?"

"I didn't plan to. You said you didn't wanna go. But she insisted we bring you along. She told me you two had made a bet."

"No we didn't. I never shook your hand."

Without slowing or turning to look at them, Sombra said, "Doesn't matter. You claimed I made up the Midnight Show. I'll prove you wrong."

"It can't be a midnight show when it's already one past—"

"It's midnight somewhere in the world," she said, giggling.

"How are we gonna get there? We're not old enough to drive."

"Sure we are. We'll take the old Mercedes Legs."

"Walk? All the way to the circus?"

"It's just three miles."

"More like five."

"It's three when you cut across the fields, Will-y."

"Don't call me that."

She giggled again. It made her hair wave and bounce on her shoulders. "Then stop being such a whiny bitch."

Will had never in his life raised a hand to a girl, but right then he wanted to punt her ass like a football. "No wonder you're so skinny," he blurted out, surprising himself. "Bet you gotta walk ten miles to school every day from whatever hillbilly flyover country you call home."

Will regretted those words the instant they passed his lips. He had no idea where Sombra lived, and even if she really was from some armpit of a village, his parents had taught him only losers judged people by their roots. Had Sombra reacted with hurt or anger or any other emotion, he would've apologized immediately.

Instead, she said, "No planes fly over Merenville," and then she looked at them.

Will's belly turned to lead. "*What the...*" he mumbled, staring at her face.

"What the what? No planes fly over Merenville, ergo Merenville isn't flyover country."

"Is that your hometown?" Clyde asked.

For a long moment, Will wondered if his friend had gone blind. Then he remembered that Clyde had met up with Sombra earlier and must've already seen her face.

"Yep," she said. "The jolliest place on Earth. You heard of it?"

"Umm, nope," Clyde said.

"That's okay. It's a really small town. Can't find it on a map."

Will drew his fingers through his hair. "Sombra, why the hell are you wearing clown makeup?"

She looked at him again, and this time she grinned. In the half-light, her painted mouth resembled a gash. A thick layer of white covered her face and neck. Each eye looked out of a scarlet smudge from which wavy lines like insect legs snaked up to touch the hairline. "I'm part of the show."

"You're a clown?"

"You'll see," she said, and winked at him. The gesture made her eye momentarily vanish in the pool of red. Like it had been gouged out.

On, they plodded. Down the street and around the old graveyard. Past the supermarket and between the park and the basketball court. Across the agrocenter parking lot and through the corn fields, their phones lighting the way. Clyde and Sombra made small talk. About her homeschooling. About Merenville and its Midsummer Festival. About the circus and the saint whose name it bore. She diverted probing questions with dumb jokes, and Clyde answered each with forced laughter. Beneath the moonless sky, Will sulked.

By the time they reached the circus, Will's shirt was sticking to his sweaty back. A dull pain in his feet heralded the blisters to come. The tent stood in the field, a soft emerald light glowing from within. Parked cars were clustered around it like bees around their queen. A couple dozen of them. Way fewer than there had been earlier, during what Sombra referred to as the Day Show. As they approached the cars, Will saw the license plates had all been covered or taken off.

"This is illegal, isn't it?" Will said.

"Shhhh," Sombra hissed, pressing a finger over her lips. "We're late. They've already started. Come." She hurried between the parked cars and led them around the tent. In the circus, someone moaned.

"Here," Sombra said, crouching at a spot where a long tear in the canvas had been sewed together with loose string. She untied the entire thing like a shoelace, opening a hole big enough to crawl through. She dropped on all fours and slipped inside. Clyde looked at Will, his mouth a straight line, and gave an uneasy shrug. Then he went in after her. Will watched him struggle through the small opening, reluctant to help and even more reluctant to follow. The moaning grew louder.

"Dude? You coming?" Clyde whispered.

Damn, Will thought. He pulled aside the flap and crept into the shadows under the cheap stands. Sombra and Clyde had crawled ahead and laid on their bellies so they could watch the show from under the lowest bench. No people on the stands. Folding chairs had been arranged in a semi-circle around the center of the arena so that the audience sat within touching distance of the performers. And what an audience it was. Men and women clad in dusty red robes, their faces hidden under hoods and balaclavas and rubber masks shaped like grinning beasts. What appeared to be a dentist's chair waited nearby, devoid of occupants.

Dust swirled in the air and a murky green glow hung over everything. A stone slab stood in the center of the arena. Will couldn't get a good look at it—the audience blocked most of the view—but it seemed about waist-high and black as onyx. A figure wearing a featureless leather mask, its sex unidentifiable at this distance, lay splayed on the slab. Another masked figure, also androgynous, lay over the first, its sweaty arms doing things Will couldn't see. They puffed and grunted like swines rutting.

"What are they doing?" Clyde whispered.

Sombra used a loose fist and a middle finger to execute a pantomime Will had never imagined he'd see done with a girl's hands.

"They're having sex?" Clyde muttered, agape.

Sombra patted him on the back as if in congratulations.

Will squinted. The top figure reached down and grabbed some triangular contraption and lowered it beneath its partner's head. The other figure moaned louder. It was like no sex act he'd ever seen, and he'd watched enough internet porn to be able to identify his favorite actresses by their breasts. He scanned the audience, the dentist chair and the empty stands, unable to pinpoint what else bothered him. Then it came to him.

"Where's that green light coming from?" he asked.

No reply.

He nudged Sombra with his elbow. "Hey. Where is that—"

"There are lamps up in the rafters. Be quiet."

No matter how much Will craned his neck, the stands blocked the sight of the rafters. He couldn't shake the impression that the green glow emanated from the dusty air itself. But to say so would be mad, so he kept his mouth shut.

The sound of slapping meat echoed in the silent circus. Louder and louder. The upper figure did things, and the other figure squirmed and moaned and arched its spine. The backs of the audience formed a wall that permitted only glimpses of the action. Some deep part of Will was thankful for that.

The moans rose to shrill, undulating screams. Whether of lust or pain, he couldn't tell. Eventually, the pair slumped against each other and grew quiet, bodies glistening. The people in the audience muttered approval. Some even clapped. A clown rose from among them. The same clown Will had watched perform crappy slapstick earlier. Sombra's father. He wore the same smeared red-and-white makeup, but his garish costume had been replaced with drooping scarlet robes riddled with stains. In his hands, a dirty sheet like an old tablecloth.

The clown wrapped the two figures in the sheet. He said something Will was too far away to hear, and the two figures rose from the slab as one, wearing the filthy sheet like a cloak. With great difficulty, they shambled away and through the back exit. Seeing the uneven way the sheet rested on their bodies, it occurred to Will they didn't look like two people at all, but rather like a single conjoined creature. An article he'd read on the internet claimed that the circuses of yesteryear kept freak shows. Some of the more unsavory ones, the article implied, had never given up the practice.

The clown laid his palms on the stone slab and hung his head. His lips worked as if in prayer. The audience too rested their chins on their collars and sat still. Minutes passed. Twice, Will began to ask what the hell was going on, only to have Sombra cut him off with a "Hush."

Then the flap at the back opened, and a crone walked into the arena accompanied by a Great Dane. In her hand, a leash. On her body, no clothes whatsoever. *A mummy. She looks like a mummy from those black and white movies*, Will thought, staring at her with the same amalgam of guilt and revulsion and morbid interest one felt when looking at roadkill.

"Ugh," Clyde muttered.

Sombra clamped a hand on his mouth. "Shhhh."

"That's the stripper you mentioned?" Will asked. He tried to sound sarcastic, but the words came out weak and hoarse, like an old man's.

"Shut up and watch."

He wanted to say, *Nobody wants to watch this*, but then he thought of all the people in the audience and felt some of his innocence drain away. The crone led the Great Dane to the center of the arena and made it climb onto the black slab. She sat next to it, caressing its muzzle with fingers long and wrinkled like bird claws. She started to sing. Too quiet to catch the words or even the language used, but loud enough to hear its eerie melody. It carried across the arena and, one by one, it infected the people in the audience. Their voices rose in a humming chant that echoed through the circus and brought goosebumps to Will's arms.

Then the crone's hand crept between the dog's legs and did things there that dropped the bottom from Will's belly. "Jesus fucking Christ," he whispered. "These people are sick. What the fuck."

"It's just an act, you big baby," Sombra said, smiling.

"Fuck this," he muttered. He called Clyde's name, but Clyde didn't answer. His friend stared at the abomination on display, his jaw slack. It wasn't until Will repeated his name for the third time that Clyde's round face turned toward him. "Let's get outta here, dude," Will said.

"Baby got scared?" Sombra said.

"Fuck off, you crazy bitch."

She put her fist under her eye and wiped nonexistent tears. "Is chicken gonna cry?"

Clyde's gaze shifted between Will to Sombra.

"Dude, c'mon," Will whispered.

In the arena, the hag let out a hoarse moan.

"Please stay, Clyde," Sombra said, her hand on Clyde's shoulder. "Don't you wanna see my performance?"

"I..." Clyde muttered.

"Please. You're not chicken like Will-y, are you?"

Will groaned. "Dude, she's a psycho."

Clyde's features looked corpse-like in the green light. "Dude, I... I wanna see. What's the harm?"

Will started to argue, then punched the ground and said, "Forget it. I'll wait for you outside." He crawled back the way he came and drew wide the hole in the canvas. Despite himself, he took one last look at the dog and the naked crone, and what he saw made him taste bile and scamper outside so fast he almost fell face-first in the grass.

The sight of that final vileness kept replaying itself in his head as he walked, aimless, into the dark. He'd known there were freaks partaking in such acts. He'd even come across videos of them on certain unsavory websites, but never in his wildest musings did he consider actually watching them. He wanted to slam his head against a tree trunk until the last half hour was erased from his mind.

The circus was a glowing nickel in the distance by the time Will thought of calling the police. Those people were committing a crime that could put them in prison. *Should* put them in prison. That the dog wagged its tail and huffed in delight changed nothing. He began to dial 911, then stopped. Clyde was still there. Would be there for God knew how much longer. The cops might arrest him too. He could get in serious trouble.

"Shit, shit, shit," Will said, and hurried back to the circus. He was close enough to see the patches on the canvas and the odd green glow, when he spotted the two figures. Big, broad men, their heads made monstrous by the animal masks they wore. They were dragging something between them. He couldn't tell what it was until they pulled it through a patch of green light.

Clyde. They were lugging a dead or unconscious Clyde, their arms under his shoulders, his sneakers scraping through the grass. Will lowered his head and fled. The police. He had to call the police. He clutched his phone, not daring to unlock the screen lest he alert the maniacs with its glow. Sombra was behind this. Had to be.

Darkness everywhere. He kept looking back. Clyde and the two men were gone, replaced by a hundred noises he hadn't noticed before. Wind whistling. Crickets chirping. Bats fluttering overhead. A muffled chanting, somehow still audible even though by then the circus had shrunk to the size of a toy car.

"I'm far enough now, I'm far enough," he whispered, unlocking his phone. Its glow sent square-shaped lights drifting across his vision, reducing everything else to a black void.

His hands shook so badly it took him four tries before he got the three digits right. His finger was moving to the *Dial* icon when a red-and-white banshee charged from the starless dark. He glimpsed long limbs and longer hair and eyes framed in crimson pools, and then something struck his wrist and his phone fell from his hand. He gasped and stumbled back, reaching for his hurt arm. His fingers came away sticky and wet. Sombra seized a fistful of his shirt and yanked him into her knife. He twisted, felt a prickle in his belly like a bee sting, and lost his footing. She was on top of him the moment he struck the ground, her hair spilling on him like a funeral shroud.

"Can't let you miss the show, Will-y," she said. "You're the main attraction."

Will screamed. At the edge of his vision he saw his phone shining in the grass and grabbed it and swung it like a rock. The screen shattered against her face in a rain of shards.

He hit her again. And again. She grunted and fell off him, her hands on her face, the knife nowhere to be seen.

Will rolled onto his side and clambered to his knees. The phone's screen was mostly gone, but the backlight still emanated a soft glow. He shone it on the grass until he saw the bloody knife glimmering. They stood up at the same time. He thrust the knife out like a fencer keeping an opponent at bay. Almost casually, she swiped her hair out of her face and smiled at him.

That was when he saw.

"No!" he heard himself shriek. *"No, no, no, no!"*

The thing that wasn't Sombra anymore reached as if to embrace him. He swung the knife. Felt it bite into flesh. Watched her stumble back, her hands pressed to her chest, black seeping between her fingers.

Will ran. He ran and ran and ran, and for what felt like a long time his mind was as dark as the night he sought to escape. He didn't remember dropping the knife or his phone, but they were gone by the time he emerged on a narrow road. He stopped under a streetlight to catch his breath and that was when he saw red stains on his shirt and all over the leg of his jeans. A shallow gash gaped on his wrist, and blood flowed down his arm. Inkblots swam before his eyes. Headlights in the distance. Getting bigger. Blurring together.

The ground rose to meet him.

***

Six years passed.

Will sat in his mother's old car, holding the steering wheel with one hand and thumbing the radio buttons in search of a decent station with the other. A college freshman returning home for the summer, he drove with his elbow sticking out of the open window and his hair blowing around his face. The night was humid and windless, the sky a drab black field. Every now and then, another car sped by.

The headlights caught a road sign in the distance. Will paid it little heed until he realized it was an exit ramp warning. He frowned. He'd driven this way a million times during the past year, yet he didn't recall ever passing an exit ramp here. What would it lead to, anyway? No towns nearby.

Then he saw it. Not so much an exit ramp as a country road attached to the main highway at an almost ninety degree angle. Unlit and unpaved, the road led into darkness. A small guide sign stood at its side. It had been planted so far from the highway, Will had to squint to read the text.

His foot slammed the brake. Tires screeched and the engine groaned. The stench of burnt rubber touched his nostrils. He put the gear in reverse and returned to the exit ramp, staring at the sign and the road beyond. Trembling, he took his phone and checked his location in a maps app. It detected neither the exit ramp nor the country road. His gaze wandered to his wrist, where a pale scar clashed with his tanned skin like a brand. There was another scar on his belly, hidden under his shirt. The belly one was small—just a knot of ragged skin—but that was where Sombra's knife had bit the deepest.

Six years ago, Will had woken up to find his arm, head and midsection wrapped in bandages. His parents, a doctor, a nurse and a sheriff's deputy were all standing around his bed. They told him a local woman had found him lying by the road, passed out from blood loss. The deputy asked when was the last time he'd seen Clyde. Will told him everything. About Sombra. About the Midnight Show. About the men who'd carried Clyde away. He omitted only one detail. The detail he'd never speak about to anyone.

They found Clyde's body later that same day. It had been discarded in a cornfield, and the farmer who discovered it didn't immediately recognize it as human. Bruises on his wrists and ankles indicated that Clyde had spent his last hours strapped into something. A large chair, perhaps.

For years, Will had wondered what would've happened if he'd managed to call 911 before Sombra attacked him. Or if he'd remained conscious long enough to tell someone what happened. As it was, the circus had already left town by the time he woke up in the hospital. Vanished during the night. A manhunt across seven states yielded no results. None of the audience members were ever identified. The cheap posters plastered across town were the only proof the circus had been there at all.

No records existed of a Saint Armenides or a town called Merenville. Fabrications all, made up by Sombra or some other psycho. The circus was a front for a cult that performed live snuff shows. Everyone believed that, and so did Will. He made himself believe it for six years. But no more.

Hunched in his mother's car with his damp hands clutching the steering wheel and his breath hissing between teeth gone dry as bricks, Will knew he'd been mistaken. What he'd seen on the night Clyde died hadn't been a hallucination. Because right here, beyond an exit ramp that shouldn't exist, set by a country road that couldn't be there, stood a sign with *Merenville* printed on it in narrow black letters. The jolliest place on Earth. A town no plane had ever flown over.

A face had been painted over the letter *M*. White with a grinning red mouth and red smears around the eyes. A clown face that no sane clown would ever wear. Will half-expected it to come alive. Just like the paint on Sombra's face had done. The phone's glow had illuminated her, and he'd seen the paint flowing and changing, the red lines drawn on her forehead coiling like tentacles. Her eyes had turned to pools of white and her irises into black pinpoints, and when she grinned, her lips stretched all the way to her ears and her teeth were like those of a lamprey.

Will put the gear into first and stepped on the gas. The car lurched once, twice, then rode smoothly into the night. In the rearview mirror, the exit ramp shrunk to nothing. Then all that remained was the lonely highway and the starless sky and the vast black void reaching to the horizon and beyond.

About the Author

Mijat Budimir Vujačić is an economist by trade, storyteller at heart. He is a published author of three horror novels written in Serbian: *Krvavi Akvarel, NekRomansa* and *Vampir*. His stories appeared in *SQ, Devolution Z, Crimson Streets, Encounters, Acidic Fiction, Creepy Campfire Quarterly, Under the Bed, 9Tales,* and *Infernal Ink* magazines, as well as in professional anthologies *Toxic Tales, Silent Scream, The Nightmare Collective* and *The Worlds of Science Fiction, Fantasy and Horror Vol1*. He believes a strong work ethic is the root of all success, and that it is best to err on the side of action. A fan of all things horror, he is also an avid gamer, hobby blogger, hookah enthusiast and a staunch dog person. He lives in Belgrade, Serbia. You can reach him via e-mail: mbvujacic@gmail.com or follow him on twitter at twitter.com/MBVujacic.

Pint Bottle Press
99¢
DOUBLE-BARREL
HORROR
A HOLES
PUNK ROCK
RE-ANIMATOR
CHAD LUTZKE

Punk Rock Re-animator

by Chad Lutzke

We're sitting in the car, in the parking lot of some old bar that doesn't look like it's been open for years. But it *is* open. And there's a band inside playing, and my friend is trying to convince me that it's gonna be great, that I've got a big surprise coming to me.

"The energy!" he says. "You can't beat it. It's like being high."

He says going to a punk show is like getting stoned — it opens your eyes, and you're never the same again. Starts a whole new world. I think he's full of shit, but I'm a good friend so I listen anyway. I listen to his rants about top-40 music and his praise for the underground. And I relate to none of it.

I'm not that big on music, to be honest. I'll listen to the radio when I'm driving to work, but I'm not out at the record store flipping through vinyl and hanging posters on my walls.

While we're in the car, I ask Mike why we aren't inside watching the first band. He tells me they suck, and it would only ruin the experience, that we need to wait.

After a few cigarettes and a half hour conversation on which chick's shower we'd sneak into if we could turn invisible, Mike says he can tell the first band is done playing and it's time to go in.

When we get out of the car, a kid comes up to us. He's probably fourteen, and he's holding a skateboard and his head is shaved, except for a big chunk of hair right in front that covers his face if he lets it. He hands us this little booklet thing that I think is a brochure at first and asks if we want to buy a zine. I look at it. It's a poorly photocopied thing with crude drawings of skeletons on the front. One of the skeletons is giving the finger, another is playing guitar, and another is on a skateboard doing some kind of trick. At the top it says *BURNT CEREAL 50 cents*. Mike gives the guy fifty cents and tosses the magazine in the car.

"Gotta support the scene, man." Mike says to me, then heads toward the club.

There's a guy at the door who's taking five-dollar bills from the people in line. I pay him, and he asks me how old I am. I tell him I'm twenty. He puts a big black X on the back of my hand with permanent marker, then takes a five from the person behind me, and the line moves through the door.

The inside of the club has this whole suitcase-traveled-around-the-world thing going on. Stickers, flyers and graffiti cover nearly every inch of every wall, beam and door in the place. The chaotic mess does give it some character, like a sweet, old lady with too much lipstick.

There's about two hundred people in here, a sea of leather and denim held together by haphazardly sewn patches and capped with multi-colored hair that stands out like confetti on black tar. Spiked hair, shaved hair, short hair, dreaded hair and tall hair, with who knows what keeping their hair standing up. Mike had a mohawk once, used to put egg in it. I love the guy, but come on. Eggs?

Mike is nudging me and pointing out girls he thinks are hot. None of them are.

"You're shallow, dude. Can't you look past the hair and makeup?" he says to me.

I shrug and look at the last girl he points out, picture her with long blonde hair instead of the shaved mess she's got going on. Can't do it. It's just not my thing, and now I understand the scene even less than I did before we walked in.

We get some sodas from the bar. The chick working it looks like she doesn't belong and can't wait to clock out. She smiles at me, and now we've got something in common—I don't want to be here either. I make a note to ask for her number after the show if I get another smile.

Mike and I sip on the sodas, people-watch, and wait for the next band. One guy in particular catches my eye. He's on the hefty side and has a short, bleach-white mohawk. He's a dirty mess, and I feel like if it weren't for the cloud of smoke I could probably smell him from here. His leather coat has metal studs on the shoulders and upper back. They look like they could cause some pain—even to himself. And there's a large patch on his back. I can't make out the band name—I'm not even sure it's in English—but the rest of the patch is a black and white silk-screened picture of a Mexican with a poncho and large sombrero. Makes no sense at all.

I look at the bartender girl, hoping to grab her attention for that second smile. She's busy serving and doesn't look my way. Finally, this guy walks out on stage, and he's all dressed in some 70s getup like he doesn't know what year it is. He's got a long, stringy beard that touches his chest and he starts reading from a book like some beatnik. Some people are heckling the guy, telling him to get the hell off the stage, but he ignores them and continues reading.

Most of what he says I pay no mind to, but then my ears hang tight to the last little bit: "But tonight I would like to think of one man, a lone individual, a man without name or country, a man whom I respect because he has absolutely nothing in common with you. The man is myself. Tonight I shall meditate upon that which I am."

Hearing those words, the man claiming individuality like that, nonconformity. They hit me surprisingly hard. And right in that instant, I get it. Not a note has been plucked, not a drum beaten, and not a scream through the mic, and yet I understand the strange hair and the outrageous garb, the piercings and tattoos, and the righteous anger. I barely have a chance to process it at all before the band takes the stage, the guitarist plugs in and feedback shrieks through the amps for a good thirty seconds. And the strange thing is, it's a pleasure to hear, that feedback. As loud as it is, it's a reminder of what the voice of punk rock must stand for, a ceaseless roar in the face of injustice, an unrelenting scream in the face of corporate sheeple, corrupt government and The Man.

And then it stops.

For two full seconds there is silence, then the band explodes, electrocuting the crowd into a frenzy of leather and spikes, sweat and fists. The singer, with dreads down to his ass yet balding on top, launches from the drum set, into the air, lands, then joins the crowd as they throw their fists in the air, chanting the lyrics in unison as they congregate around the vocalist. They reach for the mic in his hands, as though it holds a power too much for just one man. Together they sing as the vocalist thrusts the mic in the faces of random people, giving punk rock communion.

I'm a bit surprised at how much I'm getting off on it all. Twice I almost go into the circle of kids slamming against one another, dancing. But like a kid too shy to ask a girl to dance, I stop myself.

Mike heads in, his arms flailing about. The circle is full of near misses as people dodge fists, elbows, knees and feet. A guy in tight, black pants with leopard print sewn into them falls on the ground. People pick him up, never missing a beat like it's just the natural course of things—a swarm of ants working together amidst the chaos.

Then I see this guy standing there just outside the circle. The guy sticks out from the crowd, like he thought there was church tonight or maybe a town hall meeting. He's got his hair slicked back and parted on the side and he's wearing one of those sports jackets with the patches on the elbows, like some college professor in a movie. He's not even watching the band. And I can't tell if he's some pervert or if he's looking for his kid in the crowd, because the guy is just checking everybody out—looking people up and down, at their faces, their bodies.

So I'm watching this square, and he pulls out this green glow stick and pokes a chick in the bare leg with it, but she's wasted, and it doesn't faze her with all the slamming and what-not. Then he goes and sticks the fat guy with the mohawk, and that guy jumps back like he just got zapped by a live wire or something. That's when I realize it wasn't a glow stick at all, but a syringe. But it's not glowing anymore. Because it's empty.

Now mohawk guy is looking all around like *what the hell just poked me,* and I'm looking around, and nobody else is seeing this. I'm worried about Mike because he's still out there in the middle of it all. So this time I don't hesitate and head in there. I'm getting bounced around everywhere, trying to get Mike's attention. I'm tugging on his shirt and yelling, which is pretty much what everyone else is doing too, so he doesn't notice me. I look at the professor guy, and he's got a little notebook out, writing in it and watching drunk girl and mohawk guy, who is now lifting up his shirt and checking his side.

I can't get Mike's attention so I shove him, hard. He loses his balance but falls against the wall of people forming the circle. He's got a shocked look on his face, and I can see him saying "What the hell?!" but can't hear him.

I grab him by the arm and lead him outside the crowd and yell in his ear. "There's a guy in there poking people with a needle."

Mike looks at me like I'm nuts and doesn't say anything, like he's trying to figure out if what I said is really what he heard. "A guy poking people with a needle?"

"Yeah. I saw him stick two people in there. He's got a syringe, injecting people. That guy right there."

Mike looks where I'm pointing. Professor guy is looking at his watch, then looks at the girl, then looks at his watch again, then back to his notepad. The girl is still clueless. She's standing right next to the stage, bouncing up and down with the music.

"Injecting them with what?"

"I don't know. Drugs?"

"Why?"

"Dude, I'm just telling you what I saw. Maybe it's nothing."

"Did he stick that guy?" Mike points at mohawk guy who is now picking at his side, a scared look on his face.

"Yeah, he did."

Out of my peripheral, I see the girl hit the floor, like her knee gave out or something. I look at her leg, and it looks like my arm would when I used to hang it over the back of the chair in school, cutting off my circulation.

No. It looks worse than that.

Her leg looks like my grandpa's legs, but worse still — every vein bulging, throbbing. And the veins are spreading right in front of me like lightning under her skin. People are starting to take notice now. They can't help it. The chick is flopping all over the floor. And I feel bad because her skirt is riding up over her hips and resting on her waist like a belt, and she's got men's underwear on. Tighty Whiteys. But they're only white for a minute because she starts pissing in them. They fill up, and urine spreads all over the floor, getting everywhere. The band stops playing, and I can hear her skin slapping on the wet ground, splashing urine on the people closest to her. She's like a fish out of water flopping around like that. People are screaming and pointing and gasping, but nobody is helping her. Nobody wants anything to do with the piss and the veins and the flopping around.

Except one guy.

Mohawk guy walks up to her. Well, it's more like a stagger. He's not walking right. Not at all. And my guess is that under all that leather and denim is a healthy amount of purple-black veins, like lightning. The guy reaches her and kicks her good in the side, like enough to move her a few feet—hydroplaning on the piss.

At first I'm thinking that someone needs to help this poor girl, get mohawk guy away from her. But then she stands up quicker than she fell and knees the guy right in the crotch. There's a collective gasp from the people watching. The guy doesn't even flinch, but I think every other guy in the club does.

I look at the professor guy, and he's got this look on his face, wide-eyed and grinning, like he's ringside watching Holyfield and Tyson. He's all into it.

The chick knees the guy again, and I swear I hear a wet crunch. Then the guy wets his pants and the chick slips in her own urine, ends up back on the ground, clawing at the guy's legs. The purple-black veins are making their way up their necks, and their eyes are red and bulging, like there's too much pressure and they're gonna burst any moment.

The guy raises his foot and stomps down hard on the girl's leg right where she was injected. His foot mashes right through, like kicking a pumpkin two weeks past Halloween, just pulpy mush. I figured she'd be screaming and hollering but she's not making any noise at all, except a little grunt as she swings her other leg around and spins on her back, like some breakdance move, then buries her booted foot deep into the guy's side. Again, pulpy mush. The guy doesn't even budge. The boot just sinks in.

By now, people are losing their minds, but nobody wants to stop the fight. We're all scared. Ain't nobody touching these two. I catch the professor again, and he's taking notes. He takes out a vial—it's got that same green glow—and he's loading up the syringe again. All I can think is how a minute from now somebody else will be covered with bulging veins and piss, flopping around on the ground. So I run at professor guy and shove him as hard as I can. He slams against the stage, and the needle flies from his hand. I watch it spin and flip like it's in slow motion, and I'm scared the thing is going to stick into someone. Then it hits the stage, bounces and lands inside the drummer's bass drum, buries itself in a couple pillows in there.

And for one quick moment I think, why the hell are their pillows in a bass drum?

Then the professor guy straightens up and yells: "You fool!" He's yelling something about his grandfather and carrying on his work and that it had only just begun. Then he pushes through the crowd and leaves.

Meanwhile, these monstrosities are still going at it. There's skin and muscle and blood everywhere. Mike mumbles something about this being worse than a G.G. Allin show, and I have no idea what that is.

I don't think anyone realizes that professor guy is responsible for this mess because nobody tries to stop him. They're too busy running or staring at the pulpy mess and the girl with her boot stuck in mohawk guy's side. He's clawing at her leg, and though he's breaking skin and there's certainly blood, her leg isn't rotted and weak like the other.

Now, I'm not sure anyone in here has the sense to call 911, but then I see the bartender chick on the phone, her mouth moving frantically. Man, she looks good. Dark hair, giant brown eyes, these little laugh lines above the corners of her mouth.

I hear a loud splash, and the crowd lets out this horrific cry like they'd just seen something they wish they hadn't and how will they ever forget it. I look, and drunk girl has tugged her foot out of mohawk guy's body, bringing with it the guy's whole mid-section, and it's just a flap, swinging open like a rubber door. Everything that used to be inside is now on the floor and on the girl's legs—blood, intestines, and fat that reminds me of custard, and I know I'll never touch the stuff again.

The place is about half as full as it was a minute ago, with most people deciding they can't handle this shit and need out. I'm not sure why I'm not one of them. Even Mike is gone. This is much more than morbid curiosity. It's like I'm stuck. I went from being high on music with a newfound love for the scene to this surreal experience that'll probably end me up on meds for life.

But I stay. And watch.

Two guys with shaved heads and hooded sweatshirts jump on mohawk guy, who now probably weighs half as much as he did when he walked in. One of the hoodies has mohawk guy in some kind of sleeper hold, pulling him back while the other guy is laying into him with his fists—in the face and the side of the head. Mohawk guy's eyes are just looking at the ceiling like he's not even interested in what's happening, like he's not really there. But something is building up inside him. His veins are bulging more, his eyes bugging further. And I think the guy is just going to explode, when the skinhead throws another punch and mohawk guy loses his jaw. It doesn't loosen or dangle. It's just gone, like if you were to punch one of those wax figures in the museums. And if they were full of cranberry sauce and teeth.

Pieces of the jaw hit the nearest people, some on the ground, and some on the stage, inside the bass drum, nestled in the pillows with the glowing needle that started this whole mess. Then the guy hits the ground, and he ain't moving anymore.

The girl stands up, and she does a pretty good job of it considering half her leg is gone. She screams like she's on fire and lunges for the door. She doesn't make it far before her leg just kind of crumbles. She hits the ground, and her other leg breaks at the hip, bends back behind her.

This causes more than a few people to get sick, adding to the ridiculous amount of human liquids sprayed around the club. And that's when professor guy runs back in. He stops at what's left of the woman's body, then checks his watch. He starts coming at me, a real fast walk like those old people in the mall early in the morning. When he gets up to me, he pulls out a gun and points it at me.

"Where's the solution?" he says.

I put my hands up—what else am I supposed to do? And I tell him I don't have a clue what he's talking about.

Then he says: "The formula. You made me drop it. Where is it?"

I point to the bass drum with the pillows and tell him it flew in there. He looks at the bass drum, and I feel like if I could read his mind, he'd be thinking *what the hell are those pillows doing in there?*

He gets up on the stage, pulls out the pillows, then grabs the needle. Those who are still in the club are watching professor guy, but steering clear. Nobody wants to get stuck with the needle.

The guy comes back up to me and says "How long have they been dead?"

I tell him not long. Then he yells at me: "Exactly how long!? How many seconds!? Estimate!"

"Probably ten seconds before you came back in," I say.

"Okay, good." Professor guy goes over and sticks mohawk guy in the back of the neck, then heads over to what's left of drunk girl and sticks her too. He looks at his watch, grabs his notebook and writes something down. Then I hear this slapping sound, like a wet mop hitting a floor. It's mohawk guy trying to get up but he keeps slipping, and he's getting tangled in his own entrails, stepping on them. After struggling for a bit, he's able to stand up and starts walking, real slow like. Meanwhile, the chick starts pulling herself along the floor, leg stumps dragging behind. Both are making their way toward professor guy who's got this huge smile on his face.

"Come along now. Let's get you cleaned up. We've much work to do."

Before heading out the door, professor guy stops at the bar and sets down a small stack of twenty-dollar bills, apologizes for the mess, turns toward the stage and says: "Great band. Reminds me of early Black Flag," then leaves.

Moments later, I hear sirens in the distance and think about how Mike told me that tonight would change me, that there's nothing like the energy of a punk rock show. While I'm sure he had none of this in mind, I'm afraid it left a bad taste in my mouth. I'm not sure the scene is for me after all.

And then I hear the feedback.

I look at the bartender chick. She's counting the bills professor guy left behind. She stops and looks at me, and smiles. I head over for another soda, and a phone number.

Holes

by Chad Lutzke

And there's Ms. Levy, like clockwork, out getting her morning coffee. I can't tell what kind, not from up here anyway. The binoculars may allow distance, but walls stop my inquisitive eye. The beverage is lidded before she exits the cafe. I can't tell if it's black or creamed, though I assume it's heavily flavored. Not that it matters, but it's the little details I find pleasure in.

People-watching; I see no kind of perversion affiliated with it. Call it a hobby—something to pass my dying days. I make friends with the people down below. The relationships are one-sided, yes, but I get to know them regardless. And while that may paint the picture of a lonely existence, I can assure you, I am content. I've lived a long and fruitful life. I'm merely a joyfully observant fellow. Some watch birds. I watch people from the safety of my third-floor apartment.

When I bought these old field glasses, I set myself some guidelines. No looking in the windows of the apartment building across the way. Private matters happen behind the doors and windows of the residents, and those folks should never have to worry about the peering eyes of me or anyone else. Looking in cars and stores, however, completely legal according to my code. If something is going on in public, then it's all eyes up for the visual taking. But the private home? Taboo. And for the last ten years I've stuck to that rule.

Until one hot evening last summer.

***

I swear the son-of-a-whore spent his days just lurking, looking for the defenseless, the weak and the helpless. Manny Stevens was the name his parents gave him, but the kids around here preferred "Fanny." For obvious reasons.

In truth, Fanny's mother actually *was* a whore. That wasn't metaphorical. She turned tricks on Washington Avenue in the early 80s, leaving her only son home alone night after night. Rumor has it he'd be alone days at a time. I'm not even sure Manny knew who his father was. It could have been any one of the men who'd stop in for a weekend, sometimes even nesting in the house for a good six months, others barely long enough to stain the sheets.

I suppose an environment like that can certainly pave a seemingly inevitable path, but I come from the belief that when we reach a certain age we have every option to get off said path, to become our own person despite the damage done. But Manny stayed consistent in his hate for people–even into his adult life–and never veered. So when I saw him tied to a table and bleeding that evening I think a smile may have formed upon this weathered face.

***

I'm not sure what initially caught my eye enough to break my code and invade the privacy of the occupants across the street. Nothing in particular, really. I've lived here over thirty years, and I've seen the blinking glow of television sets, lights clicking on and off, the flicker of candlelight, even strobe lights one year during Halloween, and another year in the late 70s with that godawful music. But not once did anything catch my attention enough to intrude, so to look over and see Manny Stevens strapped to a dining room table wearing nothing but the suit God gave him, I was a bit taken back. Thirty years with the code, thirty years abiding. Then Manny.

I'm thinking maybe destiny, or perhaps a reward for minding my own business for so long. Lord only knows what I could have been watching with these binoculars. Lord only knows. But I never would have anticipated the sight of those exacting revenge on the neighborhood bully.

At first glance I thought I was witnessing some abnormal escapades of a sexual nature. Men these days can't seem to appreciate the warmth of a creamy thigh without the need to toss in pain or dominance or even piss for crying out loud. I thought such was the case. But then I recognized Manny by his eyebrows. Or *eyebrow*. He had one, straight across. And if there was ever anything Fanny got picked on about—other than his name—it was that eyebrow. Now I'm not one for men to be making changes cosmetically—tanning or manicures or surgical procedures and the like—but I'd certainly be an advocate for Manny plucking a hair or twenty from between those shifty eyes, make himself a bit more presentable. He already had his personality (or lack of) demonizing the rest of him. No sense in pouring salt in the ugly wound.

So there he was, strapped to a dining room table by ropes and belts. Two figures huddled over him. It looked like Manny's face had taken a fist or two, his nose bloodied. Seeing him like that was like looking at a snapshot of karma you thought would never come. But this was karma being cocky, karma showing off.

Ladies and Gentlemen, behold! Manny Stevens in a most compromising and vulnerable position. Vengeful pornography for your darkest viewing pleasure. Just like you've always wanted, deep down inside.

I think most of us wish for bad things to happen to some people at one time or another. To witness someone get a flat tire after cutting you off in traffic. Someone landing on their face after recklessly rushing past you, bumping into you without apology. Oh, the great satisfaction of witnessing it. We *want* it to happen. But the moment we see them humbled, we often change our perspective, expressing empathy as our once-vengeful hearts of stone soften with sympathy for them.

However, sympathy is not what I felt as I watched the two figures slap naked Manny Stevens with the looped metal end of a fly-swatter. I had no feelings at all, though had sweet Quincy still been sitting beside me on her little dog bed, perhaps I'd have thought different. Perhaps I'd even get help for poor Manny. But the moment he'd killed Quincy, a part of me died with her. And a bit of my heart blackened that day too, I suppose

I've relived the moment over and over again. Manny standing across 32nd Street, a treat in his hand, calling Quincy to come to him, to cross strategically, ensuring that my poor baby would be taken from me by at least one of several cars passing by; the look of satisfaction on Manny's face as Quincy breathed her last. The demon bastard.

Just as I'd decided to be done watching Manny's torture and retire for the night, I recognized one of the figures. It was Ron Berryhill. He and his friends had been on the receiving end of Manny's abusive tongue—teasing Ron for his portly size, stating that no girl worthy of a kiss would dare look twice at him, that he should head south and run until forty solid pounds were gone. And then to keep on running because those teeth of his would scare the girls away anyhow. Yes, Ron *was* rather large, but he was a good kid. I'd seen him help Ms. Levy with the door on the regular, running errands to the store for his mother. Even taking his younger brother with him at times, wrestling playfully along the way.

I watched for a while longer as they beat Manny with the flyswatters—near harmless, considering, if you ask me—

until I'd dozed off and woke to find the lights out across the way. I said my goodnight and slept soundly, dreaming of Quincy.

***

I woke in a bitter mood. I'd just spent hours asleep thinking Quincy and I were still a team. I took some solace in knowing Fanny got what was coming to him last night. I picked up my trusty binocs and headed for the window. The apartment was too dark inside. I wouldn't be able to see anything until after dark, once they turned a light on.

I spent the rest of the day like I always do, woodworking. I suppose some would call it modern-day whittling. I'd made it a hobby of mine—drilling, sanding, cutting and carving into wood with an electric Dremel, be it driftwood, scrap wood, or a healthy branch. I'd carve all manner of things. That day I had continued work on a chess set for my friend Louise.

Before I knew it, the sun sank behind the buildings and the apartment grew dim. That's when I remembered Manny. And his predicament. I cleaned up my mess, placing the Dremel bits in their case, brushing off the wood dust that covered my lap, and vacuumed the area. I peeked out the window across the street and saw no light, save for a dull glow pouring out from what I assumed was the kitchen. With the binoculars I could just barely make out the dining room table and the silhouette that lay stretched upon it.

I tossed a pot pie in the oven, set myself a plate, and got a glass of milk. I sat in my chair near the window and waited for the spotlight to shine on Manny Stevens and his suffering. Just before the ding on my oven went off, the light went on across the street. I grabbed the binoculars. Manny's face was covered in rusty, dry blood, his eyes red and swollen from crying.

This time I could see the face of the other person who'd been there yesterday. It was Tina Sullivan, the young girl who'd accused Manny of raping her. The whole thing went to trial, but because of a ridiculous technicality, Manny walked away. He went into hiding for a while, was spotted a handful of times and roughed up at least a few of those times. Even his house fell victim to backlash by way of eggs, toilet paper, slashed tires; stuff like that. Eventually the rage turned to calm and life returned to normal for Manny, though after losing his job I hear working anywhere nearby became quite the impossibility, and so he resorted to working one town over as a cashier in a hardware store.

Tina was holding something in her hand, but I couldn't tell what. She'd touch Manny's pale skin with it, and with each tap Manny would stiffen, his teeth gritting. I imagine he was screaming pretty loud in that apartment, and for a while I wondered if the cops would ever get called, and if so would they bother doing anything or turn a blind eye and pretend nothing was happening. Nothing that wasn't deserved.

I watched them poke and prod at Manny for another twenty minutes, Tina mainly focusing on the man's genital area — exacting a punishment that never was but should have been. I was about to head for bed when I watched Ron Berryhill cut Manny's thumbs off with a pair of wire cutters. A surreal moment that looked fake. Until the blood poured. I became nauseated — but only for a moment — then somehow content, calm, almost happy that Manny now spent every moment in regret. Regretting the rape, the bullying, the verbal and physical abuse … the death of Quincy.

By 8:30 I was asleep, rather heavily, until my bladder woke me around midnight. After emptying it, I checked the apartment across the street. Had I become obsessed? A sadist even? What kind of man watches another man receive such torture? I reminded myself that Manny was no man, but a monster.

I lit a candle beside the window. Quincy's little stuffed bed sat on the sill. I still hadn't the heart to move it. She loved watching the traffic below, birds on their wires, pedestrians making their way to the store. She'd watch it all. Just like me.

The light across the street was still on, and to my surprise there was a third party who had joined the others. Even before I used the field glasses I knew who it was: Mrs. Molgaard. I could tell by the grey bun she forever wore on the top of her head. I suppose if another were to attend the torturous intervention then Mrs. Molgaard's presence should be expected. When Manny was younger he'd forced Mrs. Molgaard's son, Matthew, to hold tightly to a rather large firecracker while he lit it and ran. When the M-80 exploded, it took the young boy's pinky and ring finger and most of the meat from his palm, destroying the muscle and tendon that ran through his thumb. While the thumb remained on his hand it was forever useless, a lifeless digit in the way. Up until that day, Matthew had used those small fingers to manipulate the keys of a piano with unparalleled talent for his age. So there she was, Mrs. Molgaard finding pleasure in pain. Manny's pain.

I don't need to tell you just how bizarre the whole ordeal was. Three crushed spirits gathered in an apartment, desperately attempting to fill a hole Manny had carved into each of them. And now he lie stuck to a dining room table, his own urine and feces drying under him—sweat, tears and blood pouring at regular intervals.

Initially I thought Mrs. Molgaard was there to do nothing but express her hate vocally, as initially she only paraded around the table, pointing; her face reddening, straining from boisterous cries. But then she held a nail steady on Mr. Stevens' kneecap and drove it down into the man with a quick pound from a hammer.

I could no longer stand idly by and watch. I knew I needed to do something. Before heading out the door, I grabbed my Dremel and its case of attachments. I had a hole that needed filling too.

About the Author

Chad lives in Battle Creek, MI. with his wife, children and far too many dogs. He has written for *Famous Monsters of Filmland, Rue Morgue, Cemetery Dance* and *Scream* magazine. His fiction can be found in several magazines and anthologies including his own 18-story anthology, *Night as a Catalyst*. He has written a collaborative effort with horror author Terry M. West, *The Him Deep Down*. In the summer of 2016, Lutzke released his dark coming-of-age novella *Of Foster Homes and Flies* which has been praised by authors Jack Ketchum, James Newman, John Boden and many others. Later in 2016, Lutzke released his contribution to bestselling author J. Thorn's *American Demon Hunter* series with *American Demon Hunters: Battle Creek*. And winter 2017 has seen the release of *Wallflower*, a story about addiction, delusion and flowers. Chad can be found lurking the internet at www.chadlutzke.com.

Pint Bottle Press
99¢
DOUBLE-BARREL HORROR
There Will Be Angels...
MARLENE THE MAGNIFICENT
JOHN BODEN

There Will Be Angels...

by John Boden

Train sat in his bed and hugged his ankles tightly. He embraced himself as if he were the mother he never had or couldn't remember. His ragged fingernails bit into the swollen flesh. His ankles ballooned out over the shoes that were now at least a size too small. His seeping toes poked out of the canvas. He'd cut through the tough cloth with the lid from a can to allow them some room. He blew on them, and the flies buzzed away like wishes.

Train looked around his room. His world. The crayon on the walls. Looping circles like eyes. The pictures he drew with shaking hands were taped to dirty drywall like proclamations. Hundreds of years ago, some people thought the world was flat, Train's world was shaped like an L. Plywood and dull paint, bloodstains and drawings; these were his borders. His fences. His womb.

So long he'd been tied to this bed; chained, actually. The links wrapped around the iron radiator and then around his waist, secured on both ends with large padlocks. The bed sheets were so crusty with dirt and stain that flakes of dead skin and dandruff from his foul hair looked like a dusting of snow. If he held his breath, he could hear the mites eating. It sounded like Rice Krispies.

Train sighed and looked toward the window. It was covered with cream-colored masking tape, and the sunlight made it through but in a highly diffused manner. It still hurt his gummy blue eyes. Train slid over to the edge of the bed. Rusted springs groaned, and the bones of his little back cracked and popped like firecrackers. He remembered seeing fireworks once, when he was very small. He smiled and remembered his missing teeth. The smile smothered and died and fell to a frown. His tongue darting into holes in his gums like an eel. His stomach growled.

He looked up at the high ceiling. The fly strips hung from the chandelier. Husks of insects stuck to them like promises. He allowed his gaze to trail the room. The dust-shrouded pictures, the kind in frames, on the wall. The fireplace had never burned. Not while he was there. It was filled with a mound of used litter and empty boxes. He looked at the desk and the cans. There were only seven left. The yellow cat on the label licking its lips. "Nice kitty," Train whispered and licked his lips. They split a little, and he tasted his own sour blood. His stomach growled again.

The thing in the chair looked like a Halloween decoration. That was The Man. The Sir. He was the man who had picked up Train as he walked home from school, said Train's Mom was stuck working late and had asked him to give him a ride. The man brought him here. He said they'd have fun and play games. He said so many things but none of them were true. He came in one night to sleep with Train, but his chest hurt. He sat in the chair to rest. His face burned red and his breathing sounded harsh. Sometime in the night it stopped altogether.

Train would have been frightened were it not for the angels. They kept him company.

The first angel hung on the wall nearest the cellar door. Almost to the ceiling. Her hands bound in beads and her back to him. Her head was bowed and slightly turned sideways. She prayed with closed eyes. Another had her hands flat on the walls, on either side of her head, like she was laying down, only standing up against the wall. Silly. She was so pretty, even though Train could not see her face. He just knew it. Angels had to be beautiful.

The third one had her teeth on the wood frame of the door jamb. She looked like a beaver and this made Train smile. She had a shiny metal rod that stuck from her skull. There weren't any little white worms on her anymore. Her dress was covered in dark stains. A strand of pearls dangled from her little hands with a little cross on the end.

There were other angels all around the room. One was close to the floor, her knees bent like she was praying. There were two others nearer the ceiling. They were either nailed to the wall or hung by rope or wire. They surrounded young Train and kept him safe. His army of angels, assembled by the Sir to protect him. "Angels," he mumbled and hopped from the bed. He reached up, fingers almost touching the toes of the angel above him. He grazed the rosary and caused the cross to swing like a pendulum. Train stared until it stilled. He wished he'd known her when she was just a little girl.

He looked at the large rectangle painted crudely upon the wall. Tall as The Man, it had a small black oval drawn midway up the one side. "This is the only way out," the man had said after painting it.

"What is it?" Train had asked.

"The cellar door. Through there is a strong foundation and escape." The man had sighed and tossed his paint brush into the corner. "The only way."

That was so long ago. Train was still and stared at his angels. In minutes, he fell asleep and ran through fields in his dreams.

He pulled open the can and licked the lid. Greasy and salty. He tossed it to the side and began scooping out the cat food with twisted fingers. It was delicious. He didn't bother to chew. He belched and licked the juices that coated his forearms and chin. He was out of water and very thirsty. He looked at the mountain of empty water bottles in the corner. He picked up the one nearest his foot and opened it, sucking the tepid dribble of water that remained inside. He dropped it and picked up the mildewed carton beside his overflowing litter box. The picture of the boy on the back looked a little like him, only chubbier. He dropped it, causing something to scurry beneath the newspapers and rags that lined the floorboards.

He crawled back into his bed and laid down. He pulled the ratty quilt up over his rancid self, inhaling his own reek from its moldering fabric. "In a number of days, you will be an angel, too," said the sweet voices in the dark. "We shall soar." In the darkness, near the ceiling, twinkling eyes. His angels watching over him.

"I do hope so." Train slurred as he fought to keep his burning eyes open. He was soaked with sweat and it stung his eyes. "I want to be. I want to fly," he smiled. "I want to watch over someone." And then he drifted off.

A bird hit the window with a sharp thud and a small shriek, Train smiled in sleep thinking it was his small heart.

The frail light disappeared until all was black.

His snores and the buzzing of flies became as one.

The angels never moved, the air never moved. Things crawled and chittered in corners and under trash.

There was a tiny click as the cellar door opened but a crack.

Marlene the Magnificent

by John Boden

The cul-de-sac was hopping on the afternoon of little Timothy Brushett's ninth birthday. The streets were paved with Scions and Escalades. BMWs and Mercedes. The sun hung mid sky and bathed all in cheery warmth and bright light. As children played in the yard and on the sidewalks, a breezed danced about them.

Inside the home of the birthday boy, his parents Lucy and Brock carried bowls full of chips and pretzels into the living room and placed them on paper-covered end tables. Two-liters of soda and jugs of juice lined the bar. The grill was warming up on the patio for hotdogs and burgers. The dining room table was heaped with colorful boxes and gift bags for the lucky lad.

Lucy took a sip of her beer and looked to Cherice from next door. "I still can't believe we were able to get her." She chuckled nervously. Cherice drained her bottle and smiled. Lucy went on, "The waiting list was weeks long, but luckily Brock works with her cousin and somehow jumped the line."

Cherice nodded and swallowed a mouthful of goldfish crackers. "Have you seen her act before?" she managed. Lucy shook her head as she strode into the other room with another bag of snacks and a bowlful of grapes.

They heard the squeak of brakes and saw a car pull into the end of the drive. It was an old station wagon. The sides were painted to simulate wood paneling so faded it looked a bit like marbled meat. One of the rear tires was a donut, and a piece of white poster-board taped to the door read in large shaking script: *Marlene The Magnificent*, surrounded by doodles of bunnies and butterflies.

"Oh my God! She's here! She's here!" Cherice gasped and bounced up and down, clapping excitedly like a schoolgirl who just made the cheerleading squad. Faces, both large and small, pressed to the windows and peered at the new arrival.

Marlene checked her face in the rearview mirror. She used an old napkin to wipe the bit of lipstick from her teeth. She arched her back against the cracked vinyl of the seat and unhooked the seatbelt. Leaning forward she reached under her denim miniskirt and worked off her panties. She wadded them into a ball and tossed them into the backseat with the rest. She sat up straight and adjusted her blue halter, her nipples poking out like little thumbs. She took a final drag on her cigarette and dropped it into the open bottle of soda sitting on the console. A small hiss told her it was out. She coughed and wiped the phlegm from her tongue with the napkin and tossed it in the back with the knickers. "Showtime."

The front door burst open with a kick of what was once a mighty fine leg. Still taut and muscular but now traced with spidery veins. Her toes were painted silver and she wore an anklet of shell. Marlene sauntered to her spot in front of the fireplace, where a large red tarp was spread over the floor. "Happy Birthday Tommy!" she sang, a smile so unrealistic and large like an alien poised to attack. The father closest to her leaned over and whispered. "Sorry, Happy Birthday Timmy!" she apologized and took a bow. All eyes were upon her. "You guys ready for some amazing shit!?" she said, aware of the slight slur to her speech. She didn't care. The gunfire of applause and childish giggles told her the answer. "Let's get fucking started."

Marlene sat down on the floor, tarp crinkling like wrapping paper. She shimmied back against the hearth and lifted her hips to slide off the denim that pretended to be a skirt. She was naked from the halter down, her pubic hair shaved into the shape of a little top hat above her slit. She shook out her hands with a little more drama than needed. Her bracelets jingled and her rings gleamed in the sunlight. She found her edges and pulled herself open a little. Like pulling little elephant ears.

"For my first trick" she said, wheezing a little as the position grew more uncomfortable the older she got. She smiled wide and slowly began rubbing herself with a bony finger. Once she was moist, she worked it inside and then the next. Once she got three in, she pulled them out and held between them something blue. She continued pulling, revealing a handkerchief that was tied to another then another then another ... red to green to yellow ... and it seemed to have no end. She had been doing this for so long that the faces and stares barely registered. She only had eyes for the check at the end of the gig and the smokes and booze it would buy her.

After what seemed like endless minutes, she pulled the last of the cloths from her snatch. As the children hooted and clapped and the parents whistled and cheered, she wadded them into a ball and tossed them over to the left. They stuck to the wall.

She asked one of the grownups for a drink and while she waited told a few jokes. "What's black and white and red all over?"

"A sunburnt penguin" offered a little girl with pigtails.

Marlene shook her head. "Nun with a head wound!" An explosion of laughter as she drank her ginger ale. She looked down at her cooch and noted that it sort resembled half a tomato … on its way to going bad. *"Your little man in a boat has turned into the old man on a trash barge,"* she thought. She frowned and then caught herself, turning that frown upside down.

"Another!" she announced, "And I'll need a helper for this one." She pointed at little Timmy, who sheepishly shook his head. "Oh C'mon, Birthday Boy," she pleaded. His father pushed him a little and he came forward. "I like your watch," Marlene cooed as she patted the boy's rosy cheek. "Is that Snoopy?"

"Yeah," he whispered.

"May I borrow it for this trick?" she smiled, and he took it off and handed it over. "Thanks."

She took the watch and slid it between her lips, once she had it spit slick she took it out and slid it between her other lips. She then moved her hands away and reached to her left to remove something from her bag. "Here Timmy." She handed him the hammer. "I want you to hit me in the twat as hard as you can." She rested her hands on her knees and closed her eyes.

Timmy swung the hammer. Not all that hard the first time, it sounded like someone dropping a spoonful of pudding on the counter. Almost a splat. She grimaced and then allowed it to stretch up into a smile. She nodded, and he swung again and again—three times in all. Marlene opened her eyes and winced a little. "Thank you Timmy, you can sit down."

Her voice was shaking a little, but she felt it safe that she was the only one who'd noticed. She grabbed a towel from her side and dabbed at her cooze. A little blood, not much.

She then licked her trembling fingers, reached inside herself, removed the boy's watch, unharmed. "Ta-da!" she called and the boy came back for his watch. "Safe as milk," she said and kissed his forehead. As the parents and other children clapped and called and laughed and whistled, Timmy sat in the corner, sniffing his watch.

"You're gonna love this." She coughed as she stretched the balloon between nicotine-stained fingers. She smiled a wide and red-rimmed smile and pulled open the mouth of the balloon. She held it down to her cunt and began rolling her stomaching. There was a hissing wheeze of a sound, like air escaping a deflating air mattress or pool toy. The balloon began to inflate. Filled with queef, it grew and lengthened. She took the finished product and tied its end. With a few twists she had a two-foot long rubber schlong with two rotund balls at the base.

"That looks like Kevin Bacon's dick, blue and squeaky." She smiled and handed it to Cherice who blushed but licked it anyway. Marlene picked up another balloon and repeated the feat.

After the Chinese linking rings and the milk glass trick, she did a few card tricks and told some more jokes. The kids were particularly fond of this one: "What's green and smells like pork?" She was certain they didn't get it but mainly laughed at the Muppet connection in the punchline.

It was time for the closer. This one always knocked 'em dead. "Well, guys, I've had a great time today. Have you kids had fun?!" Marlene asked. The response was louder applause and shouts of "We sure did!" Little Timmy was still in the corner, watch under his nose like a time-telling moustache. "Well, then I have one more trick for you…"and with that she leaned far back and began rubbing herself.

She worked her fingers in again, then her whole hand, to the wrist. She made exaggerated faces as her wrist turned and rolled. Her brow furrowed and she finally gasped and shouted, "There you are!" Bracing one hand against the hearth brick, she slowly began to pull the other hand free from her cunt. The first thing to come out were the ears. White fur, slightly slimed but fur nonetheless. She pulled a little more and the little head came out, followed quickly by the front paws and body.

She held the rabbit up for the crowd and they all stood up, clapping and hollering. Marlene dropped the dead bunny to the floor and stood herself. Thin trickles of blood circled her bare legs and calves. She took her bows and reached down to pick up the dead rabbit. She put it in her purse and started packing up as the children and parents began to attack the spread of food and snacks.

Marlene waved goodbye and wiped the bit of icing from her lips on her arm. She ducked into her car and started it up. She sat there for a moment and looked at herself in the mirror. She fumbled for a Newport and then with the lighter. As the mentholated smoke filled the car, she looked at the drooping ears that hung from her purse. She'd have to get home, wash that damned rabbit and get it back to the neighbor boy's hutch before they got home. She didn't need another run in with them. She lit a cigarette and pulled away from the curb.

About the Author

John Boden lives a stone's throw from Three Mile Island with his wonderful wife and sons. A baker by day, he spends his off time writing or watching old television shows. He likes Diet Pepsi and sports ferocious sideburns. His work has appeared in *Borderlands 6, Shock Totem, Splatterpunk, Lamplight, Blight Digest,* the John Skipp edited *Psychos* and others. His not-really-for-children children's book, *Dominoes* has been called a pretty cool thing. His other books, *Jedi Summer with the Magnetic Kid* and *Detritus in Love* are out and about.

Pint Bottle Press
99¢
DOUBLE-BARREL
HORROR
BLACK ROCK BOYS
THE PERFECT FIGURE 8
SIMON DEWAR

Black Rock Boys

by Simon Dewar

"What do you think it is?"

The three of us—Joey Spader, Arturo and I—were standing in a clearing atop a wooded plateau that, on a whim, we had decided to explore. Before us rose a fluted stone column of the deepest midnight. Creeping around its circumference and up the entire length of it, were strange silvery runes or hieroglyphics of some kind. It didn't look like any language I'd ever seen, and none of the symbols looked like pictures of anything I recognized.

"The fuck should I know?" said Joey, adjusting his baseball cap. We were boiling in the afternoon heat, and Joey, short tempered at the best of times, was on a hair trigger. "It's old though. Real old. Looks Greek or Roman, what with those lines that run up the sides."

I stepped in for a closer inspection. "Didn't think there was anything out here. Think it's like … a totem or something? Thought all the Indians were further west." My voice trembled slightly. The stone was unnerving. Alien. I felt some kind of affinity with it, as though I'd seen it before, perhaps in a dream. Or a nightmare. And yet I felt an attraction to the stone, like a magnetic pull.

"Native Americans, *guero*." Arturo said. "They're called Native Americans these days. But they lived in tents and shit back then. They weren't known for masonry," he said, walking in a slow circle around the stone. "Man, look at this thing. Just look at it. This is like some Stargate shit, man."

I wanted run my hands over the rock's strange markings.

"C'mon," Joey said, tugging on my backpack and forcing me back a step. "We gotta climb back down the ravine and set up camp."

I snapped a quick photo with my cell phone, the flash briefly illuminating the trunks of the trees around us. The captured image flashed up on my screen. It was distorted. The black column was just that, a rectangular smudge of impenetrable blackness, framed by the over-exposed long grass and the trees behind.

***

Ideally, we'd have gone west but we had only the weekend. It was a shame the Rio Grande was so far away because it was beautiful in summer. Instead, we'd left early, hiking east of Tularosa, in a forest bordering the Mescalero Apache Reservation.

We'd chanced upon the black rock several hours into the woods and, after concluding our investigations, we climbed down the ravine from the plateau, and hiked to a small lake nearby.

"So what's up with you showing up at the last minute? We'd almost left but then you rocked up," Joey asked as we walked.

"Do I need a reason?" I said, not wanting to tell them Dad had practically forced me, and too hot and exhausted to concoct a decent excuse.

"Sure. Everyone needs a reason," says Arturo. "What's the matter, brosef? Ritchie hassling you again?"

Ritchie Vance was ringleader of the schoolyard thugs and a star player for the Tularosa Wildcats. He was a musclebound jerk with a perpetual chip on his shoulder that he seemed to delight in taking out on whomever seized his fancy.

"No," I say.

"Is it a girl thing?"

"Maybe. I don't know." This time I was straight up lying.

"It's Bella," Joey said and laughed delightedly. "You totally went there didn't you, you dumbass."

Arturo, putting on his best circus ringmaster voice, didn't miss the opportunity to take a dig. "Ladies and Gentleman, step right up. Here we have the biggest *pendejo* in Tularosa High. Not content with monthly beatings from the school bully, he gonna start messing with his sister too. Stare into the face of the dead man walki—"

"Shut up!" I said. "I didn't mean anything to happen … but those legs, man…"

"All right, brosef. All right!" Arturo laughed.

We grinned. We smirked. We giggled. Three sixteen-year-old boys, celebrating my first sexual conquest. High fives were had.

In truth, I'd been following Arabella Vance around like a lovesick puppy for almost an entire year. She was 5'10, all legs and had the smoothest dark tan I'd ever seen. She had every male eye on her when she strutted through the school halls. Ritchie—her brother—knew it too.

We arrived at the lake, and I stripped down to my boxer shorts and with a *whoop!* jumped into the cold water. Within minutes the other boys had joined me, and we laughed and splashed and *ewww'*ed at the muddy sediment between our toes.

"Ahora que, hermanos?" Arturo mumbled sometime later as we floated on our backs. "Where to from here?"

"Back to camp," Joey said, his arms waving beneath the surface of the water to stay afloat.

"No, I mean in life, *amigo.* One more summer and we're done. Me? I want to go to college. Maybe some Ivy League school. I'll study history and meet some shy girl hiding her beauty behind thick glasses and turtlenecks."

"You're after a naughty librarian, Arty?" Joey said, laughing.

"No. Someone good to take home to mama."

"I'll probably wind up working in Dad's shitty corner store and never make it further than Las Cruces or Alamagordo," I said, shaking my head. I'd all but given up at school and any thought of college. I'd spent so long chasing Arabella, now that I had her I felt like I'd had a rug pulled out from under me. In truth, I was lost. Looking for a direction. Looking for hope.

"What about you, Joey?" Arturo asked.

"Who knows? Don't ask hard questions. Anyway, we better make camp soon, Don Vito. We can make the fire and roast us some s'mores."

"I'm Mexican, asshole, not Italian."

"He knows," I said, and we all laughed as we paddled to the shore.

***

The sun threatened to plunge below the tops of the trees, and the shadows about us lengthened like creeping hands. We were close to camp when we heard a voice from the trees ahead.

"Who's that?" Arturo said.

"I can't tell but they sound familiar," Joey said, cupping his ear to listen. "They're young. Sound our age."

"Can you see them?" I asked. The light was fading fast now, and I squinted through the trees, trying to locate the people speaking.

"Not yet, they're headed this way."

"I got a bad feeling about this. We should split," Arturo said, urgency gripping his voice.

A twig snapped ahead. We bunched close together behind a tree.

"They came this way, I'm sure of it," a familiar voice said. It was Jayden Thule, one of Ritchie Vance's friends.

My mouth went dry and I wanted to gasp for air, but forced my diaphragm to keep my breathing slow and shallow.

Jayden was a wiry tough kid who spent his time fishing and shooting and camping, rather than playing football or chasing girls in town. For all his traditional manly hobbies, he was a straight-A student who delivered perfect poetry recitals in English class and probably turned as many girl's heads as Bella did boys'.

Someone else spoke. "Then let's hurry. I want to find that piece of shit." This time, there was no mistaking the angry bitter voice of Ritchie Vance.

"Meet back here when they're gone." Joey whispered, side-stepping from tree to tree and off into a thicket to our left.

I grunted, and turned to look at Arturo only to find he'd already disappeared. I stood alone, peeking from behind the tree. I could see them clearly now. Jayden gazed at the ground, studying the broken twigs and disturbed leaves that marked our trails in and out of the camp site. A hunting rifle was slung over his shoulder.

"You want him that bad, huh?" Jayden said, squinting at the leaf litter. "For just talking to B?"

"Not just talking, you idiot. I saw her phone. She's been sexting him for weeks. Sending him photos of herself in her panties."

"He's probably fucking her."

"Just fucking find him. Did you forget how much I'm paying you? Or aren't you the big hotshot hunter you claim you are?"

Jayden grunted and adjusted his baseball cap, looking speculatively at Ritchie, as if wondering if he were worth the trouble. I leaned against the tree with one hand for support, trying not to make a sound. My hand slipped tearing a chunk of bark away from the tree with a loud crack. I lost the battle for balance, falling to one knee.

Jayden shrugged, looking for all the world as though he'd rather be somewhere else. "Found him."

"Stay there, you piece of shit!" Ritchie hollered, but I was off, already back on my feet and hurtling into the forest.

My feet flew, and the trunks of spruces and aspens whooshed past me, kissing my skin with their branches. I was blowing like a racehorse, but my arms and legs kept pumping. Something odd came over me, coaxing me, pulling me in its direction. Before I knew what I was doing, I'd begun the ascent back up towards the plateau. To the black rock.

Behind me, I heard Ritchie cursing as he followed. Jayden would be right beside him; he knew how to move through the woods better than Vance, who was too much of a spoiled townie.

I was halfway up the ravine when they emerged from a thicket. Ritchie let out a murderous howl at the sight of me.

He yanked at the .308 slung over Thule's shoulder. Jayden tried to hold onto the strap, but Ritchie pulled the gun out of his hands. He wasted no time bracing the stock against his shoulder and taking aim.

The rifle barked and the round ricocheted off the rocks behind me, showering me with splinters of stone. My heart lurched in my chest, but I pushed on to the tree line where the ravine met the plateau above. Behind me Thule was cursing Vance as they ran.

I burst through the brush into the clearing, almost tripping over my boots, panic squeezing the air out of my lungs. I scrambled towards the black column.

What was I doing here? What was I thinking?

"Stay right there, motherfucker. I've got you now!" Vance's shout echoed up the ravine. He was almost at the tree line, Jayden's hunting rifle in hand.

The intervening space between me and the rock disappeared, and I wrapped my arms around the engraved obsidian mass.

"Help me! Please," I cried, my fingers digging into the etched and whorling runes that spidered over the ebony surface. The markings were hot under my hands and the stone spoke, a grating sound like two colossal slabs of granite sliding over each other.

—*Child, I am Immortal. Everything I say is true*—

And in that very moment I was born again anew.

***

I later found that Joey and Arturo managed to grab our gear from the campsite before Vance and Thule returned. They searched frantically for me in the surrounding thickets, before giving up and starting their long trudge back home.

I had been infused with purpose, with a hunger for knowledge of Him—for the power that He promised and the secrets He would reveal to me; for the immortality I might taste in the shadow of His black being. Lying groggy in my bed, I swallowed, wondering how He had plucked me from the woods and returned me safely to my house in Tularosa.

I rose and dressed myself for the day to come, secure in the knowledge that I was now the scion of something old enough to make the measurement of time itself irrelevant.

I slept that evening and The Father filled my mind.
—*You shall be three*—

***

I strode into the schoolyard, bag on my back, cocksure smile upon my teenage face. The glare of the sun didn't stop anyone from turning their gaze upon me. Everyone stared. News had spread—perhaps of me and Bella, perhaps of what went down when Ritchie and Jayden stalked us among the trees. People knew *something*.

I made my way through clusters of other kids who chatted in the yard. As I passed one friendship circle of girls, I heard the whispers. Chrissie Makin batted her eyelashes at me. Joanna licked her lips. Mary Jane blushed furiously and looked away. I kept walking.

In the distance, I saw George Christenson and Jayden Thule standing by the water fountain. Christensen was talking, but Thule's inscrutable eyes were locked on me. In that moment he seemed appraising and contemplative, as though sizing me up for something. I felt a sudden urge to speak to him, as though the events in the woods created some kind of bond between us. The bell rang and reluctantly I broke eye contact and hurried to class.

Math class that day was a mid-term calculus test with Mr. Duran that I hadn't prepared for. I sat in my chair and drew out my pencil, eraser and calculator, dimly aware that the test papers were being handed out and that Duran was issuing the usual warnings about how many percent of our overall mark rode on this one test, and how those who were found to be cheating would be suspended if not expelled.

I felt no fear, no nerves. There were no butterflies in my stomach or cold sweats that usually heralded an impending academic non-performance. Mr. Duran placed the paper on my desk, looking briefly at me above the rim of his glasses. His eyes narrowed. My eyes narrowed, looking back at him. He opened his mouth as if to say something and then he shut it, moving off along the aisle to hand out the rest of his test papers.

I looked at the test paper and felt The Father's gift upon me. The shapes and graphs on the paper writhed, opening themselves to me and imparting their hidden secrets and insights. Rates of change and the slopes of curves revealed themselves to me with Newton-esque ease. With the stroke of my pencil I perfected the accumulation of quantities and divined the areas under and between curves. Cos, Sin and Tan were as a trigonometric trinity through which I derived, with full certitude and correctness, all that must be known of Year 11 calculus.

Five minutes later, when I was done, I placed down my pencil and waited.

***

Arabella saw me in the hall after class, and her long-nailed fingers pushed me into a corner behind some lockers. She was beautiful as always, a flowing mane of chocolate hair framing her oval face with its perfect symmetry and immaculate makeup. Her eyes were wide, a band of white bordering her deep emerald irises.

"Baby, you're in trouble," she said, her breathing coming shallow and quick. "My brother knows. He found the pics I sent you. I think he can put two and two together."

In my head, I heard Ritchie's howl and the .308 round whizzing off the rocks behind me. Felt my heart skip a painful beat just as it had in the ravine.

"Yeah, I know," I replied and grimaced. "Guess everyone knows, given how they were looking at me when I walked in today."

"Yeah they know, but … it's not just that." She said, grinning coquettishly and drawing her painted nail along my jaw. "You look different."

"Different? How"

"I dunno, baby. Taller. More confident. Sexy."

"Why thank you," I said, willing my body not to respond as her curves pressed up against me.

"I better go," Bella said. "I'll call you. I gotta get a new phone. Ritchie broke mine." She blew me a kiss and turned to go, her hips swaying as her pumps rap-rap-rap'ed back down the hall.

My phone buzzed, and I pulled it out to read the message. I didn't recognize the number but it could only be Ritchie: *Today or tomorrow. It don't matter. Your dead.*

I was stuffing my phone back into my pocket when Joey grabbed me by the collar and pulled me from behind the lockers.

"You son of a gun. You made it!" he said, clapping me on the shoulder.

"Somehow. Glad you did too."

"I thought he'd freakin' killed you or something. Heard a gunshot. Me and Arty bugged out real quick. Arty almost called the cops until I talked him out of it. If we found out you were dead we could talk to them then. And if you weren't? I ain't no snitch. Anyhow, I lugged all your gear back to my house, but I was so wrecked I couldn't drop it by. I tried to call yesterday. Your phone was off."

"I'm lucky he missed, man." I said, grimacing. "Guess he's built heavy for football 'cause he couldn't catch me. And don't worry, I was wrecked too. Don't even really remember getting home, just waking up in bed."

"No shit." Joey said, then looked back over his shoulder in the direction Bella had left. "You seen Ritchie? Heard he's looking for you."

I glanced around the throngs of kids making their way through the hall. "No, but I'm trying hard to fly under his damn radar."

It was important that I take care. I had just begun my journey. My new life. What did The Father have in store for me? What was possible now?

"Holler if you see him. I'll keep my eyes peeled too, but it'll only be a matter of time before he finds you. Wanna hook up after school? I stole half a carton of Becks from my old man and I've got nothing better to do."

That afternoon I would be busy. I would trek east to the black rock and throw myself again before it.

"I can't. There's something I need to do."

"Yeah, yeah," Joey said, rolling his eyes. "Just don't get caught again, eh?"

***

I took a different path home. Part of it was embedded street smarts; the knowledge that the usual route presented the best ambush chance for Vance. Part of it was that tugging sensation, the same one I had experienced that lead me into the ravine and up to the plateau.

I thought of Arabella as I walked. I had dreamt of her for more than a year, and now that I finally had her, what now? Did she really mean anything to me? Was she the trophy girl, the attained-unattainable? Or, was the thrill of being with her more about the thrill of defying Ritchie? The questions seemed almost irrelevant now that I'd found Him.

As I made my way down the backstreets and through the long grass beside the turnpike, I thought only of The Father. The gift He had bestowed upon me for my worship was immediate. My perception grew and widened, and the secrets of material existence tickled my consciousness, letting me know that the vistas of creation would be widened for me further still. I picked up the pace.

I was maybe a mile from home when I heard the yelling. The tugging seized me, propelling met towards the sound. Two people came into view. It was George Christenson and Arturo. And their fists were flying.

Arturo threw the wild haymakers of a kid doing everything he could to fend off a much larger and deadlier opponent. Christenson, of a similar height but stocky, ducked and weaved with the skill of a seasoned schoolyard bruiser. Every now and then, his big fist would thunder forth. When Arty was lucky, it would glance off his raised forearms or his shoulders and he could roll with the punches. When he was unlucky, it would rock his head back violently, eliciting a string of Spanish expletives and furious backpedaling to momentary safety.

Arturo was slowly and methodically being thrashed, and yet … I felt no fear. I felt no anger, no adrenaline dump that usually presaged the start of a fight. I felt no great concern for Arturo's safety or health. Instead I was at peace, filled with a surreal sense of calm and confidence. I shut my eyes. The Father was with me.

The first bird that swooped at Christenson was a black-tailed grosbeak.

The second was a cooper's hawk.

Within moments Christenson was being circled by a flock of all kinds of birds, taking turns to claw and peck at him, the fury of their squawking and the flurry of the beating wings creating a tremendous cacophony. He screamed, windmilling his fists in the air, just as Arturo had only moments earlier. A few seconds more and he broke into a run, careening towards the nearest cluster of houses.

Arturo gaped at the fleeing thug, then turned to look at me. "Did you fucking see that? *Dios te salve, María!* That was some biblical shit, man!"

"You okay?" I asked, knowing the birds were no mere coincidence and feeling the tugging sensation reorient my being towards the black rock. Towards Father.

"Yeah I'm okay. A little banged up, but I'll live. Fucking Christenson, the *puto*," Arturo said, spitting in the direction George had fled. "Didn't say shit, just came out of nowhere swinging. Probably trying to earn points with Vance because I'm friends with you."

"Shit, Arty. I'm sorry." I said, as he wiped some blood from his lip and gingerly pressed at his face. He was covered in sweat from his ordeal.

"You don't be sorry. You didn't do nothing wrong. But if you could get Bella to put in a good word with Chrissie Makin for me, I'll sure take it."

The connection—for I now knew that's what it was—to The Father pulsed, telling me what I must do.

"You don't need Bella to put in a good word for you," I said, smiling.

"I don't?"

"Nope," I replied. "Not once you hear what I have to tell you." I put my arm around his shoulders. We walked. And we talked.

***

I told Arturo everything. I told him about being chased and shot at by Ritchie, of the black rock seething to life as I flung my arms around it. Of Father speaking to me, and of waking up in my bed as though nothing had ever happened. I told him of the promise of worship I had made, and of the gifts imparted to me.

Arturo smirked at first, and then as I—a boy from Tularosa, New Mexico—began to explain advanced calculus in minute detail, he stopped. He listened and toyed with the fine gold crucifix at his neck. "You aren't shitting me, are you."

"Nope." I said, squeezing his shoulder. "He's inviting you to him. I'm going to him now. If I hurry I'll probably even be there and back before Dad gets home from work."

"What about Joey?" Arturo said, frowning.

"Joey doesn't need him," I said.

"Why me then?"

"That you might worship and revere him, a timeless being of great power. And so he may reward you for it."

"If he's so powerful, why's he need us to worship him?"

"He doesn't, but what's the point of great power if no one fears and respects it?"

"Why not reveal himself to everyone then?" Joey asked, the crucifix now enclosed in his clenched fist.

"Because when everyone has something, it has no value. Because he's the ineffable; the inscrutable; the unknowable. Because if he were to reveal himself openly then so would his peers. And why me? Why us? Because we need him. Because we're the proverbial wet lettuce, Arty. We live life on the run from assholes like Vance or Christenson, too afraid to stick up for ourselves. You want to get a real education—but what chance do you have of that Ivy League school you're dreaming of? *Nada.* You want something more than just working at a Chuck E. Cheese's or an Applebee's—but we ain't got no prospects, bro. We got nothing."

"You've got Bella."

"I got lucky. And what have I got to give her? You think she'll stick around once she sees the first college sophomore in his varsity jacket and shiny car?"

I knew that dreams of an Ivy League scholarship and that pretty bookworm wife were all Arty really had. Dreams, unlikely dreams, but dreams he clung to anyway. I played shamelessly on his emotions.

I felt no remorse.

Arturo tore the small crucifix and chain from his neck and cast it into the sandy dirt nearby.

"Tell me what to do."

***

The grating grumble of The Father's voice slowly faded away in the dry summer air. I watched Arturo's hands fall away from the black rock, his pupils rolling back down from behind his eyelids.

"Brother?" I asked, shaking his shoulder softly. He turned to me, eyes wide with the awe of his beatific vision. Of meeting Him.

"He showed me things. Taught me things. He knows everything," Arturo said, still coming to grips with the immensity of what he had learned in his communion.

"He has power, Arty. Power to elevate us. Power to change everything … whatever we need."

"But where is He from?" Arturo wondered. "He didn't tell me but I felt unimaginable distances stretching through time and space."

"I'm not sure he's from any*where* exactly. The Father is as he always was. As he always will be."

Arturo nodded, *ahhh'ing* softly as though my non-answer made perfect sense. "I am the second?"

"Far as I know," I say, helping him to his feet.

"Second guy who's gone down on him eh, wetback?" Ritchie spat each word like a curse, emerging from the shadows at the tree line. "How does it feel to be his sloppy seconds?" His maroon Wildcats shirt strained over his muscular frame. His hands held a rifle, different from the .308 that Jayden Thule had been carrying.

"No, no no no… *Padre nos protege!*" Arturo said, stepping back and bracing himself against the black rock.

"Ritchie," I said, holding my palms out in front of me. "Don't be stupid."

Ritchie braced the rifle, loaded it with a clicking slide of the bolt and pointed it directly at me. "Got you now. Thought you could touch my sister and get away with it, you white trash motherfuck?"

I stepped backward into Arturo and the black rock, propping myself against it.

"Thought you could make my sister your slut, and I wouldn't say boo?" Ritchie growled, stepping forward and aiming again at me.

Arturo stood straight, the terror melting away from his face. Under my hand the black rock grew hot. I stood tall, staring down the barrel at Ritchie.

There was a deafening crack and Ritchie's head exploded like a watermelon stuffed with firecrackers. Clumps of bloody flesh and bone shards sprayed across the clearing. The rifle dropped from his limp hand, and he crumpled to a heap in the dirt.

Arturo looked at me and I nodded. The Father had given judgement.

Jayden Thule stepped into the clearing. And there was a kind of perfect poetry to it. As perfect as one of his English class recitals. In his eyes was the same intent and appraising look he'd given me in the courtyard earlier that day.

"The Father is immortal and everything He says is true," Jayden said, smiling at me as gun smoke snaked from the barrel of his hunting rifle. "But did you really think He'd leave His worship solely up to you?"

***

Standing tall, we began the walk back to Tularosa, the hot summer air now cool in our mouths, our sun-beaten brows now dry. Before us the world shifted and reformed. Spruce and cottonwoods and oaks bent to create a way for us. The very rocks themselves *moved* to grant us passage. The creatures of the land, elk, porcupines, coyotes and black bears, prostrated themselves before our coming. Circling us above, cooper's hawks and peregrine falcons screamed in adulation.

The Father said it, so it was.

And the Black Rock Boys were three.

The Perfect Figure Eight

by Simon Dewar

I

Some people say death and taxes are the only two sure things in life—but I think they're forgetting about pain.

****

I've pumped up the tires on my bike and have a half dozen DVDs to swap at Blockbuster. I love action movies and superhero flicks … but what I really love—what I crave—are racing movies. *Smokey and the Bandit. The Cannonball Run. Hell Wheels.* I've seen them all. And when I'm on my bicycle—I am Burt Reynolds in the *Cannonball Run*. I am Jamie Lagarno behind the wheel of his hell machine.

I am invincible.

I have another reason to get out of the house—I want to see who's moved into the house across the road. It's a nice house, similar to our own but with white bricks. The Caulfields have moved out, downsizing to a townhouse now that their kids have gone to university. A large moving van arrived yesterday, dropping off dozens of cardboard boxes, couches, beds and other furniture. A new family has moved in.

I'm just starting to notice girls; I hope the new family is full of daughters, but it turns out they've only got one.

I step out our front door with my backpack slung over my shoulder. The heat of the air parches my throat as I wheel my bike out of the garage. It's a canary yellow 70s-something Apollo Gemini. It's a 10-speed beauty with white tape-wrapped racing handlebars and Shimano gears. I adjust my bag and swing my leg over the bike.

There's a sudden crash, and I look up and across the road. A girl is chasing a cat through the front yard. Stuck to its tail is a bright streamer tied to a cluster of tin cans. It hisses and spits, each step punctuated by a hectic rattle and clang.

The cat zig-zags across the grass but its escape is blocked by the laughing girl who drives it back toward the corner of the yard.

"Here, kitty kitty!" she says, her voice ringing out across the cul-de-sac. She herds the animal to the corner of the yard, stopping it from reaching the road. "Run, kitty kitty!" she said, her laugh a vicious bleat. The terrified animal steps backward into the corner where the fence meets the front gate. That poor cat isn't going anywhere.

I imagine my own beagle Toby bailed up and cowering from an assailant, and it's enough to loosen my tongue. "Hey!"

The girl stops and turns. The cat seizes the moment and jumps. With a screech, it's off—a hissing, clattering, blur of fur sprinting down the street.

She shoots me a death glare, blazing out from under her dirty blonde fringe. A look I'll never forget. It shocks me, 'cause at first glance, she's cute in a grunge kinda way.

"Who are you?" she asks, hands balled into fists.

"I'm Pete. I live here." I jab a thumb over my shoulder at my house.

"Well, well. I'm hurt, Petey," she says. "Are all our neighbours dickheads, or just you?" She turns to walk back towards her house, and I notice a ladder of thin white scars climb each of her wrists. "I'm Jessica," she says, an afterthought.

"That wasn't cool, what you were doing," I call back to her, with more strength than I feel.

"What do I care what you think?" She looks over her shoulder as she steps under the shade of her porch. "This is my street now."

***

The brass bell tied around the door handle is still ringing when I shove the DVDs down the chute in the counter.

"Thanks, Donny," I say.

Donny smiles, "Hey, no problem, kiddo. Y'know, I've got *Hell Wheels* under the counter for you already. This time it's on the house. What is it, the two hundredth time you've rented it?"

"For real? Thanks!" I say, laughing. I make my way through the aisles and flick through the titles on the shelves. The brass bell rings again.

With *Hell Wheels* already sorted, I am tossing up between *The Running Man* and *Universal Soldier*. What I really want is a movie pitting Arnie against Dolph Lungren, but know that I'm gonna have to choose between the two eventually.

"No. I've seen *Interview with a Vampire* a hundred fucking times, okay. Tom Cruise is like five feet tall, and I'm totally over Christian Slater. It's time to move on, Tina."

The voices startle me and I drop the DVD case I'm holding.

"Whaddya wanna get then?" another girl replies.

"Something action-y. We'll see."

I pick up the case and turn my head. Katie Lawson, my big crush, and some friend of hers are only a few metres away.

"How about...? No ... hmmm. Oh hello! —*Death Race*. And it's got Jason Statham in it too!"

I almost drop *Running Man* again. The *Death Race* remake? Really? I find myself intervening before I can stop myself.

"Hey, umm—"

"Oh hey" Katie says, turning to me and hooking her hair behind one ear. "Peter. From school, right? Didn't realise it was you."

She knows my name, oh god, she knows my name.

"Yeah. Ms. Calhoun's class. I mean … we're in Ms. Calhoun's class. Together."

Tina guffaws and Katie giggles. "I know what you mean."

My ears begin to burn. "Just wanted to make a suggestion…" I say, trailing off, keeping my eyes on Katie's face and trying to forget her friend is there.

But the blonde girl will not be ignored. She groans, rolling her eyes so hard she can probably see her own brain.

"Uh, sure. Go for it," Katie says, a small smile creeping onto her freckled face.

"Well, rent whatever movies you want, right ... but, the oh-six remake of *Death Race* with Jason Statham kinda sucks. I mean, it's *really* terrible. If you haven't seen it, check out the David Carradine original, *Death Race 2000*. It's mid-seventies old-school, but it totally still kicks ass."

Katie laughs, and for a moment I'm sure she is laughing at me. The room is unbearably hot now and my face feels like it's on fire.

"Sure," Katie says. "Why not." She turns to Tina, "You hear that, Tee? Looks like we're going old-school tonight."

Tina groans again and folds her arms, tapping one foot on the carpet. I wonder why the lights are so bright. I realise I'm holding my breath. I have to get out of here before I say or do something stupid.

"I'll see ya around," I manage.

"See ya at school," Katie says, but I'm already scuttling away, glaring at a grinning Donny as I make my way to the counter.

I fly from the parking lot at Blockbuster with all the speed my Apollo Gemini can muster. Working hard to put some distance between me and Katie. There's a skid of rubber as I jump my bike over the gutter and onto the footpath. I pedal hard, my legs pumping like pistons. The sun is bright and high in the sky, and sweat soaks my singlet. As I ride home, I *am* Jamie Lagarno locked in behind the wheel of his hell machine.

A steep hill ahead breaks down the back of the shops. Whether you're on a bike, rollerblades or skateboard, the consensus is unanimous—the hill is evil. One wrong move and you're done. But if you don't choke—*if you just hold on*—you shoot across the bridge at the bottom and over the storm water canal, like a ball out of a cannon.

My bike plunges down the hill towards the bridge below.

Am I thinking about the DVDs in my backpack, or the Palmer girl and the cat? Am I thinking about Katie and *Death Race*? Am I in my own world, tearing past rival cars at Daytona, Talladega or Indianapolis? Maybe—but later, the only thing I'll recall are the little things. Trivialities. The breeze taking the edge off the heat. The dry smell of the knee-high grass baked brown by the summer sun, as I crest the top of the hill behind the shops. I won't even remember losing control.

My life doesn't flash before my eyes and there is no Hollywood slow-motion impact. One second I hurtle along the path and down the hill, the next I'm a bloody mess smeared down the footpath like so much roadkill.

The world is now bathed in white; all sounds come as if

through dense wads of cotton wool stuffed into my ears. Everything is wet with blood—my clothes are soaked with it and my hands and knees are glossy red and sticky. My heart is a colossal drum, beating far away. I'm on the ground now; I push myself first to my hands and knees, then slowly to my feet.

Where is my backpack? My helmet's in it. Mum will tear me a new asshole if she knows I wasn't wearing it.

I squint through the stinging blood and the thick white fog obscuring my vision.

There—in the grass by the path.

I stumble over, open the bag and retrieve the helmet. My pulse pounds in my temples. I drip bright red drops of blood over the helmet, as though this will prove to Mum that I'd been wearing it. As if that even matters now. Despite the pain, I laugh, realising the absurdity of it all.

I stand for a minute—*so dizzy*—and survey the scene. My racer lies on its side a few metres ahead of a crack in the concrete path. One side of the concrete has risen to form a jagged step some two inches in height. This must be what threw me. The front wheel has come off with the force of the impact and rolled off into the grass.

The breeze, so comforting before, stings my shredded skin. I lumber back up the hill, past a playground. I blink hard and try to gather my thoughts. They elude me, swimming like slippery eels. My teeth chatter. I want to collapse in a heap but know I have to hold on until I get to the shops.

The tavern comes into view first. The empty parking lot indicates it's too early for patrons to be drinking. The white fog has receded somewhat but I squint against the sunlight.

Then I see it, resplendent in its white paint and emergency markings and flashing lights. I don't question why an ambulance is there, I only care it is. Later, I'll learn an elderly lady was having a heart attack in the supermarket.

Hope and adrenaline flood me. I run to the vehicle. The back doors are open; the ambulance is empty, the gurney gone and not a paramedic in sight. From the van's big side mirror, a ruined mess stares back at me.

Confused, exhausted, I stumble over to a wooden bench outside the tavern.

I'll just lay down there for a while. They'd find me eventually. Just need to close my eyes for a moment. *Just a moment…*

—…Jamie raises his head and peers into the smoke. His every nerve screams with the effort. He is bleeding, the tang of fresh blood in his mouth. Through the thick black smoke and tongues of flame lies the wreckage of his hell machine—a pile of mangled steel and burnt rubber. He shuts his eyes and lowers his head to the dirt…—

From the distance come shouts and the steady *slap-slap-slap* of shoes on the pavement.

***

The physical pain is nothing compared to the soul-crushing shame of having to front up at school a week later with a face full of scabs and yellow-green bruises. When the other kids see my scab-encrusted face, their lips curl in disgust.

It's not long until I'd earned the nickname 'Leper Boy,' courtesy of Jessica Palmer, naturally.

As for Jess—no one has seen, or even imagined a girl like her before. She's the talk of the school:

Do you see them scars? What an attention seeker…

Heard she got expelled from Dickson High School and she's slept with half the school…

Heard her Dad used to be a biker and he just got out of prison…

I *almost* feel sorry for her.

***

It's fifth period math class, and I am busy ogling Katie. I love her dark hair and the smattering of freckles across her nose and otherwise porcelain cheeks. Her perfect white teeth and smile are like happiness itself. *And* she actually watched the David Carradine version of *Death Race*; she's far more interesting than algebra.

I'm yanked out of my reverie by a scrap of paper bouncing across my desk.

"Pete."

I groan inside. It's Palmer.

"Pssst! Petey," is followed by, "Petey, ya window-licker!"

I look back over my shoulder to where she sits in the next row, next to Dale Morris. Since Jessica started at the school they've made quick friends. It's a match spawned in Hell, as far as I am concerned.

I make the universal shrug-and-spread-hand gesture for "What?"

At the front of the class, Ms. Calhoun has turned to the blackboard; her droning voice is punctuated by the squeak of chalk.

"You got your eye on Katie, Petey?" Jess says.

"No," I whisper.

"C'mon Petey, there ain't no shame in that. She's a real nice piece of work. Nice rack."

"Shut up, Jess." I say, toying with my calculator, trying to keep my hands busy so she won't see them shaking. Just my luck: A girl moves in across the street—a *hot* girl— and she's a real bitch.

"C'mon, I'm just trying to help," she says. Her tone feigns sincerity, but I don't believe her for a second.

"Piss off," I'm praying Ms. Calhoun will turn back

around. Praying Jess will lose interest.

Jessica's husky bleat is joined by a guffaw from Dale. They are going to do something. *No no no no no. They're going to…*

I watch as Jessica calls out to Katie. Katie turns. Her smile is dazzling. She looks at me but I look away, knowing what is about to go down.

"Hey Katie!" Palmer calls softly.

I'm not here. This can't be happening. Only it is. It really, truly, is.

Katie's raised eyebrow is the picture-perfect image of confusion.

"Seems like Leper Boy here has a real hard on for ya," Jess says. "A big scabby leper's hard on." The whole class is listening now. Dale's hooting sounds over the top of the tittering laughter. Katie's face flushes crimson and she spins back to her desk.

Ms. Calhoun turns from the blackboard and gives the class a disapproving glare. "I hope everyone is paying attention," she says in her nasal voice. "If you don't understand algebra then you'll have no hope of passing the mid-term test."

The class goes quiet and I cover my burning face with my hands.

I want to die. I want to curl up into a ball and disappear.

II

If you could find a way to bottle and sell pain, you'd make a mint. It's an unlimited resource we pour out of ourselves and then inflict on everyone around us.

***

I'm sitting in my room, dozing in front of the TV. I

haven't died or dissolved into nothingness yet, but not for want of trying.

Hell Wheels is in the DVD Player for the thousandth time. Toby is snuggled up close, his head on my lap. I scratch behind his ears, and he butts his head back into my hand. He's my best friend. Thinking about the crash, about that bloody hill, I can almost feel the wind in my hair again; can almost see the bridge at the bottom divided by those concrete bollards. Dad fixed the Gemini, but I haven't taken it out for a spin again. It's too soon.

On screen, Jamie Lagarno is head-to-head with the cyborg Road Rage. They'll both crash, ending up in a fiery wipe-out when Road Rage T-bones the out-of-control Lagarno. I'm just not in the mood. I think of Katie and desperately push my despair and mortification back into the recesses of my mind before switching off the TV.

A loud bang sounds across the street and I rush to the window, slide it open and peer out across the yard.

Nothing.

The street is dark but all the lights are on at the Palmer house. Silhouettes move back and forth behind the curtains in a commotion of light and shadow.

Thump. Thump.

"Stop it!" a woman shrieks. "She's just a kid!"

Crash. Thump. Thump.

The woman again. "Randy, please!"

More crashing. More bangs. The woman screams some more.

Great. Just great. The Palmers have brought trouble to my small suburban cul-de-sac. The commotion continues, and I try desperately to burn away any sympathy that might develop for Jess. After what she did, she doesn't deserve it.

I try—and fail. Knowing that Jessica is probably being thumped to a bloody pulp, my thoughts jumble over one another unbidden.

Who the hell would beat their own kid like that?

What could she possibly have done to 'deserve' it?

Is this why she's so mean — she's taking it out on other people? And is that even a valid excuse?

I think about the ladders of fine scars that creep up the insides of her wrists for a moment, before shutting the window and turning *Hell Wheels* back on.

The roar of the big engines and the cheer of the crowds drowns out thought. And sound. And everything.

***

Within a few weeks, I'm back on my bike. Back to fifth period math class with Jessica Palmer; and the looks; and the taunts.

I don't know who put the note on Mrs Calhoun's desk, but she pulls me aside after class one day to ask me if everything was okay. To ask me about Jess. I am vague about things, not knowing what had been in the note and not wanting to give away too much.

A few days later someone steals my shoes from the front porch of my house. Three days after that, someone at school lets the tires down on my bike, and I have to walk five kilometres home, pushing my bike in the hot afternoon sun. I spend the evening pumping up my tires again rather than watching a movie like I'd planned.

The next day at school, whenever I turn around, Jessica Palmer is right there. Poking me. Prodding me. Pointing at Katie.

"You don't have a chance with her, Petey. You know that, right? Prissy bitch probably wants someone from the football team, not a skinny uncoordinated shit like you," she says. I tell her to shut up and leave me alone, but some variant of the discussion will recur tomorrow.

I've had enough. So I tell tales. Snitch. Whatever you

want to call it.

I tell my Year Co-ordinator about Jessica and Dale. I tell her about the name-calling, assuming the school can protect me from Jessica and any retaliation.

I'm wrong.

I'm called to the Principal's office. Upon entering, I see Jessica Palmer already seated. I take the seat next to hers, our chairs uncomfortably close. It's a dusty room lined with bookshelves full of teaching manuals and educational periodicals. Weak sunlight filters through the old venetian blinds. Mrs. Kennelly is seated behind a scuffed office desk, spectacles perched proudly on the end of her long nose.

"What do you have to say for yourself, Miss Palmer?"

"It's my word against his. That's all you've got," Jess says, shooting me a sidelong smirk. Her face is as it always is, but something about the way she sits in her chair, almost gingerly, tells me she's not okay. Despite the heat, she's wearing a long-sleeve shirt under her school t-shirt, which covers her arms to the wrist.

"That's the problem, Jessica. If you hadn't already landed yourself in my office three times in the last two weeks, I might believe your word. Such as it is, I'm inclined to believe your word is not worth much."

"Aww c'mon, Miss. Don't be like tha—"

"Jessica Palmer!" Mrs. Kennelly slaps the table with a force I'm surprised she can muster. "You will address me as Mrs. Kennelly, and you will be sitting Friday afternoon detention this week and next. Now get back to class."

I rise to leave but she waves me to sit. "Not you, Peter," she said. The door clicks shut behind Jess on her way out.

"Are you okay, Peter? Do you have any questions?"

"Yeah. Sure. How about 'Can I change class?', or 'Why aren't you calling her parents in here?' Or mine for that matter…?"

"Because there is a process through which we must move. I cannot escalate this issue until Jessica has been given a chance to consider her actions and rectify her behaviour. To do so would open myself, and the school, up to accusations of unfair treatment and bullying of students." She smiles encouragingly. "I will be speaking to Jessica's parents. If the issue is recurrent, we'll have to organise a meeting with yours as well."

It seems reasonable enough, I suppose. What would I know? At least they have it all on record now, right? I say my thanks and make my way to class.

On my way, Jess and her cronies circle me in the quadrangle—like sharks around a wounded whale calf.

"Leper boy!"

"He wants to get his end in Katie Lawson!"

"Doesn't have a hope in Hell!"

"Ugly leper cunt!

Every taunt they make is a sharp little tooth that tears into me. Steals something from me. From the corner of my eye I see Katie Lawson and her friends watching, heads leaned close together, whispering. I can't breathe. I have to get out of here. My hand creeps up to cover my injured face. I die a little more inside as I push through the throng and run to class.

***

At home, I dump my school bag on the floor and hightail it to the kitchen pantry. I smear bread liberally with Nutella for my staple afternoon snack. I grab a jug of juice from the fridge and pour myself a long glass and park myself at the kitchen bench to eat. To let the rush of sugar sweep into me and let the stress of the day ebb away. I forget about Jessica Palmer, the bullying, and even Katie for a moment. When I finish, I lick my fingers clean and put my plate and glass in the sink.

"Toby," I call, expecting to see the beagle waddle into the room with his floppy ears and happily wagging tail. He doesn't.

"Hey! Toby. C'mon boy. Wanna go for a walk?" Even the mere suggestion of a walk is usually enough to bring wuffs and yips of excitement from the other end of the house. It doesn't.

I search the house, every room. I search the back yard, his kennel, his hiding spot under the back deck. He's not there.

Has he gotten out? Is he wandering around in the nature reserve at the end of the cul-de-sac? He does that every now and then.

I make my way out the front door and down the street to the edge of the nature reserve. A small laneway takes me into a forest of pine trees. Dark limbs stretch above me and block out the sun. The needles crunch under my school shoes.

"Toby. Tooobyyy," I call, and make my way past the bole of a large pine and round a crop of large stones. That's when I hear him whimper.

Behind the rocks, in front of a tree, stands Jessica Palmer and Dale Morris. Dale's face is pale, with a sickly green tinge to it. One hand covers his mouth as though he's trying to force something back down.

Jessica is standing there, a long thin stick in one hand. Toby hangs from the low branch of a pine by his hind legs. They're tied with cheap plastic braid.

"Nice of you to join us, Leps," she said.

My breath catches in my throat. I try to swallow. "Oh Toby. Oh boy." The words are thick in my throat. My face is wet.

"No time for tears, Leper Boy."

"Let him go." I'm frantic. "Just let him go. He's a dog. What'd he ever do to you?"

"It wasn't him—it was you. You can't take a joke *and* you snitched, you little turd. You want to dog me? Well, I'ma whoop *your* dog and see how you like that!"

The branch in her hand cracks like a whip across Toby's belly. Toby yelps in pain and kicks his hind legs causing him to swing violently on the end of the nylon rope. That atom of sympathy I have for Jessica splits and detonates inside me.

I scream and rush forward. Dale takes two steps back and empties his stomach onto the pine needle floor.

"Stop!" Palmer raises the stick above her head. My feet skid to a halt. "One step closer and I'll whoop him again. And then I'll whoop you too!"

I struggle to breathe. I sniff and wipe my eyes and face. "What do you want from me? What do you want, to let him go?"

Jessica gives me that baleful look—the same deathly glare from the day we first met—and then she smiles.

III

It swathes through our lives, on to those around us and then right back in again. There is no escaping pain. Just as it is unlimited, pain is also infinite. *The perfect figure-eight.*

***

My mouth fills with saliva and I swallow. I scratch the scab on my upper lip.

"You gonna wuss out or what, Leper boy?" Jessica Palmer asks. She casually picks her nose and examines the result.

"Shut up, Jess."

"Hey, I cut him loose. I kept my word, didn't I?"

I grunt, not wanting to give her any satisfaction. Boys and girls from my grade have amassed for the spectacle. Word of the event had spread fast through school. Could I really do this?

"Well? Let's see you do it then. Let's see you stop being such a goddamn pussy, Leper Boy. You asked what I wanted in return for your puppy's freedom? This is it. I want you to smear yourself down that hill again. And I want to see the fear in your eyes before you do it."

Dale is there, a little less green than he was at the park earlier.

I squint down the hill at the broken concrete, the smell of dry grass filling my nostrils, painfully aware that the bench outside the tavern that I once collapsed upon is a mere 50 metres behind me. I swallow and wipe my sweaty hands on my shorts.

I want to save face. I want to show up the smug bitch. I'll have to ride the best I've ever ridden, or better. Be the best I can be.

Or be someone else.

The thought careens through my mind like an engine out of control. I shake my head, but the thought won't quite shake free.

"I'll do it!" I say. "But you're doing it too, Palmer."

The assembled kids laugh. Jessica's face flushes. Anger flows out of me now. For the humiliation I've suffered. For Toby.

"You think you're such a fucking hotshot, Palmer?" I say. "You talk a lot of shit and you've got a real big vagina, beating up a little dog and all—but you got the guts to race me?"

The crowd ooooo's and Jessica steps forward and slings her leg over the bike. She's changed out her long-sleeve shirt, and I see bruised hand marks on her bicep, and a thin red rung on each of her laddered arms.

"Alright, Petey. I'm in," she says. "Let's see if you can keep your face off the ground this time."

I shake my head. "Nuh-uh. Not so fast. You lose, you leave me and my dog alone. That's it."

She harrumphs loudly and takes a long look at the assembled kids. The look of expectation on their faces is plain. She has no choice. "Alright," she says, finally. "You're on."

The crowd of kids cheer and jeer, and it's settled. Out of the corner of my eye, I see Katie Lawson is among them, a small smile on her lips. I catch her eye and that smile doesn't waver, and I know I'm not imagining it. I know it's just for me. But then she was gone, lost in the sea of pimpled faces and waving fists.

I climb onto my bike and shut my eyes for a moment.

—Lagarno steps into the cockpit of the great machine. For a moment, before the engine has even started, the roar of the crowd is deafening… —

My hands are sweaty against the tape on my handlebars. My pulse quickens as I place a foot on the pedals and push off. I don't take off down the hill but instead turn back. Jessica is right behind me. I circle lazy, imperfect figure-eights, and take in Jessica's sneer each time I come about.

In and out, and right back in again.

—The engine of his great machine screams as he burns past the stands. In Jamie's rear-view mirror the crowd is wild, hundreds of thousands of screaming mouths and waving hands… —

I send out a silent call, hoping against hope I'll be spared this indignity and will somehow wink out of existence.

I don't.

Toby and the bloody welt on his side creep into my thoughts. The way he'd hobbled home from the park. The way he'd whimpered and looked up at me with those liquid chocolate eyes.

I swing the bike around and angle it for the footpath at the top of the hill. My heart beats a painful tattoo. Sweat runs over my chest and dampens my singlet. I fight the powerful urge to stop the bike, to jam on the breaks, to just ride off in another direction and leave Jessica Palmer and that hill behind.

My feet hammer the pedals. I heave the handlebars and jump the gutter onto the footpath.

"Don't choke again, Petey!" Jessica crows and pedals up alongside me.

—Neck and neck, the great machines blaze a path around the track… Road Rage and Lagarno, the only contenders. Jamie winces. Through the comm feed in the helmet blasts Road Rage's bionic squeal of triumph…—

I grit my teeth as a fresh breeze blows over me and cools my sweaty body. The smell of the brown grass along the sides of the path is strong.

Jamie and I fly down that hill. The roar of Lagarno's engine, the thrum of its power, reverberate in my mind. Air whips past my ears and through my hair, and balloons my t-shirt behind me.

I no longer pedal, only try to keep my feet *on* the pedals. I don't dare look at Jessica. The crack in the concrete and the bridge below race up to meet me. I yank on the handlebars to bring the front wheel off the pavement. It drops back to the ground again after clearing the crack. The back wheel bucks as it hits. A farmyard squeal of perverted joy tells me Jessica is still beside me. I have to do something, have to shape the race to my advantage. I have to take her out.

—We— know what to do.

—The great machines speed toward the tunnel, a black mouth in the mountain that swallows the track in front of them. His own machine is redlining now, emitting a super-charged banshee's scream. The entrance is upon them. Jamie clenches his teeth, side-eyes Road Rage, and swerves into the cyborg's great machine—

Jessica Palmer's bike veers off the path, through the sunburnt grass and into the storm water canal. Her scream punctures the air. There's a splash as her bike ploughs through filthy shallow water, a thud as she slams into the canal wall.

My bike hurtles between the side rail of the bridge and the concrete bollard in the middle.

I shoot across the bridge like a ball from a cannon.

About the Author

Simon Dewar lives in Canberra, Australia. By day he is an IT consultant; by night, he writes and edits the literature of anxiety. His fiction can be found in various anthologies such as *Death's Realm* (Grey Matter Press), *The Sea* (Crossroads Press), *Bloody Parchment: The Root Cellar* and other stories (eKhaya, Random House Struik). He is the editor of the *Suspended in Dusk* anthology series (Grey Matter Press).

Pint Bottle Press
99¢
DOUBLE-BARREL HORROR
ROAD KILL
THE GETAWAY
GOW-1551
PATRICK FREIVALD

Roadkill

by Patrick Freivald

As Jim slid his hand down Gina's tight stomach and under her bright pink nurse's scrubs, she slapped it. "Ten and two, mister."

"It's a stick-shift." He eased the jet-black Mustang around the wooded bend left-handed, teasing with his right the small silver piercing nestled just below her delicate tuft of downy hair. She shifted, thrusting out her hips to accommodate. He flicked his middle finger, delicately brushing against the metal and the hypersensitive skin that contained it.

Her lips a sullen pout, she dug her fingernails into his wrist and drew his hand lower.

"Dammit, you're going to get me all horned up before work."

He smirked. "Gives you something to look forward to."

"Yeah, I'm really going to be craving the D while I'm elbow-deep in Henry Johnson's colectomy. What a turn-on."

The smirk widened into a grin as his fingers plunged deeper. "Better finish you off before we get there, then."

She gasped and slid her hands down to his, one underneath his palm to play with her clit, the other snaking behind. Her hips worked in slow circles as her fingers worked as fast as they could. Face flushed, she stared at him with those bright blue eyes, a paragon of feminine beauty with high cheekbones, full lips, olive skin and a riot of curly black hair.

"I'm going to be late." She groaned, the desperate sound utterly destroying her protests.

"We'll make it qui—"

"JESUS!"

As her body tensed, he jerked his eyes back to the road. Foot jamming hard on the brakes, he jerked the wheel hard right. The Mustang skidded with a shriek and fishtailed around the large black and red mass taking up much of the lane, then came to a halt fifty feet further down the road.

Jim stared at it in the rear-view mirror, his heart hammering. "Is that a fucking bear?"

Gina turned around in her seat and stared wide-eyed out the back window. The black shape lay in the road surrounded by a pool of congealing blood.

"It ain't a deer. Way too big."

"Think somebody hit it?" he asked.

"Or shot it and it fell there."

He pulled onto the shoulder and killed the motor.

"What are you doing?"

"We got to get it out of the road. Someone could really get hurt."

She popped her door. "Most people are probably watching the road instead of finger-banging their wife." She got out, cracked her neck. "All right, let's do this."

"You didn't seem to mind," he muttered. She either didn't hear him or pretended not to, and instead of a reply she slapped the top of the car.

"Hurry up. I'm going to be late."

As they walked toward it, he picked out details—a paw spread wide across the double-yellow line, brown claws just touching the asphalt. Definitely a bear, male and pretty big. It shifted. Jim stopped, put a hand on Gina's arm. "I think maybe we should call the cops."

"Yeah, did you see—"

Something red rose up from the middle of the mangled corpse. They shied back.

Eyes opened in the vague, worm-like shape, all too human but glazed over with a silvery film. It blinked, and Jim processed the image into something less monstrous but no more sane.

Blood covered the little girl, matting her hair and clothes into a red-brown mess. It smeared across her face, obscuring her features except for her wide-open eyes. She bared her teeth, turned and bolted—not toward them, but into the woods, leaping and ducking over logs and under branches with native confidence.

"Holy fuckballs." Gina gaped at the girl until she disappeared in the dense brambles. "Was she hiding in that thing?"

Jim pulled his phone from his pocket and dialed 9-1-1. A calm, male baritone answered.

"9-1-1. What's the emergency?"

"Hi, um, we just saw something really weird while driving. A little girl."

"Okay."

"She was, um, playing in roadkill. Ran off into the woods all covered with blood."

"Is she injured?"

"I don't ... know? I don't think so. It was hard to tell. She ran off."

"And the animal?"

"A bear. It's dead."

The dispatcher took his name and phone number, then verified their location. "All right. We'll send a car out just as soon as we can. Sit tight until he gets there."

"Whoa, whoa, whoa," Gina said, loud enough to be heard over the phone. "I got to get to work."

"Who's that with you, sir?"

"That's my wife," Jim said. "She works at the hospital, and she's already going to be late."

"We'll have someone there as soon as possible. Do you want me to stay on the line?"

Gina glared, and Jim gave her his best "I'm not in charge" shrug.

"No, man, it's cool. We'll wait for the cop." He hung up. "Sorry, babe."

Gina ran a hand through her hair, grabbed it in a fist and pulled. "Fuck. I got to call work."

A soft cry came from the woods as she dialed, in the direction the girl had run.

"Did you hear that?"

Gina held up a finger, telling him to wait. As she talked, he wandered over to the shoulder, where a deer trail led off into darkness beneath the canopy. Another cry, a high-pitched sob, came from not too far inside.

He took a step, and Gina's fingertips on his wrist stopped him.

"The fuck are you going?"

"That girl's in there. She might be hurt."

She looked from the woods to the car and back. "Fuck."

He led the way, following the deer path into the dense underbrush. They stopped to listen, heard nothing.

"Hello?" Gina said. "Little girl?"

Jim joined her, and they called out together at the top of their lungs.

"Ah!" came a reply forward and to the right. He dragged Gina off the trail toward the noise, crunching over the thick layer of leaves smothering the earth beneath.

"Hey! Stay right there! We'll—"

Heat exploded in his foot, a searing agony like nothing he'd ever experienced. He fell, half-dragging Gina with him, and writhed, unable to think of anything but the unbearable pain. He didn't know how long it took to regain rational thought, but sweat soaked his clothes, and his foot hurt—a persistent ache that shot lightning bolts of pain up his body if he tried to move it. A red haze filmed his vision.

The sun had set.

Gina stroked his hair, and he realized his head rested in her lap.

"Shhhh, baby, don't try to move. The cops should be here soon. They said it would be soon. They'll get you out, and then we'll get the fuck out of here."

He looked down, aghast at the metal jaws scissored into his foot. The crude, rusted steel jaws had stabbed right through his sneaker, and his head swam just to look at it. A chain attached it to a huge rock, where it had been drilled right into the face.

"Get it off!"

She shushed him, stroked his hair. "I can't. I pull that thing off, and you're going to bleed out before we get to the car. If I tourniquet you'll lose the foot for sure. You got to stay put until the ambulance gets here."

"How long has it been?"

"An hour."

He lay back, trying to think straight. "Why an hour?"

"I don't know, baby. Maybe they hit traffic. They know I'm a nurse and I'm here with you, and you're safe. Just don't move."

Gritting his teeth against the pain, he choked down a groan and shifted to look up at her beautiful face. Tears wet her puffy cheeks, and a glob of snot plugged her right nostril. He didn't care; he just wanted to stare at her, take in every part of her in case he never saw her again.

Under the sound of wind through the trees, the rustle of distant animals, the chirping of frogs and chattering of squirrels, a human sound tickled his eardrums: crying, pathetic sniffles and sudden sobs.

"Do you hear that?"

Gina nodded, but she made no move toward it.

"The girl, she could be in trouble. She could have stepped in a trap."

"Shhhh." Gina put her finger to his lips. "She's not your worry right now. The cops will deal with her when they get here, but right now you need to rest."

He shook his head. "No, no, baby. It isn't right. You have to make sure she's okay."

Gina snorted. "And risk stepping in another trap? You're my priority right now, sugar, not her. She'll take care of herself for the time being."

He'd always known that Gina hadn't wanted kids, but had no idea she could be so callous, so devoid of empathy.

"Jesus, honey, it's just a little girl. She might be in one of these traps!"

Gina lowered her gaze until their eyes met. Her flat expression came in handy at the hospital, giving or getting news that would destroy lives and devastate families. She used it on him only when angry or exasperated beyond measure.

"Okay, yeah. A little girl. I'll be right back."

"Be careful! Prod the ground with a stick. Shuffle your feet."

She slid out from under him, setting his head on a bed of leaves. "Don't you die on me. I'll be right back. Right. Back."

He smiled at her fierceness, her take-no-shit-even-from-God attitude. "I'll be right here."

"I'm serious. Don't try to move—if that thing ruptured an artery, you'll die in seconds if it comes loose. Just lie there and wait for me. Wait for me."

Turning his head to watch her leave, he twisted his leg the tiniest bit and had to stifle an agonized gasp. Blood filled his mouth, warm and meaty; he'd bitten his lip. The pain didn't even register, even after he'd realized it.

She disappeared into the trees, shuffling feet wooshing through the dead leaves, stick thumping on the ground before every careful step. The crying faded, and her footsteps with it.

Through the leaves, the moon crept across the sky. Animals rustled in the underbrush. Almost out of earshot, a dog barked.

"Honey?" He called out, but his dry throat and drier mouth wouldn't project. His head swam with the effort. "Honey?"

He licked his lips, tried to wet his throat with saliva, and tried again, at least a little louder. "Gina!"

Falling back to the earth, he hadn't realized he'd partially sat up. The itching burn of his foot had shot through with ice so cold it seared his flesh. Leaves rustled, the moon drifted through the trees, and still she didn't return.

Heavy footsteps trundled, snapping twigs and crushing leaves underfoot.

"Thank god. Where have you been?"

Something rumbled, a low growl, and its shadow blocked the moon. Huge, white incisors glistened in a black mouth, while flat eyes devoid of light stared into his soul from inches away. Its breath stank of shit and decay and worse things, and defiance rose in his breast. Even dying, alone in the woods, he wouldn't allow such a crude beast to kill him. Humans dominated the planet not because of opposable thumbs or big brains, but by being the meanest, most murderous motherfuckers on the savannah.

He screamed, everything he had poured into a sound of pure, terrified fury. The bear bellowed, a deafening sound that answered his fury a hundredfold. It reared, towering on its hind legs, dropped to all fours, and ran.

Jim laughed, insane relief pouring out of him in mad cackles. "That's right, fucker! You'd better run!"

The flush of relief turned to panic, squeezing his intestines into knots. Had it run toward Gina? The girl?

"Honey!?"

Nothing. The susurrus of its passing faded into nothing, and then to memory.

It had been so long. Where the hell was she?

Squirming his fingers into his jeans, he managed to extract his phone without exploding white-hot lightning from his foot too many times. Eighteen percent power, 4G, and three bars. He called her.

It rang, a series of beeps he got for every pending call. He strained his ears to listen for her ringtone, "Bad Reputation" by Joan Jett. Somewhere far away something that might have been music sounded, but it might have been his imagination as well. He hung up after ten rings, and tried again. And again.

Snarling, he disconnected and dialed 9-1-1. It picked up on the second ring, the same pleasant baritone that had answered an eternity ago.

"9-1-1, what's the emergency?"

"Hi, I called earlier about the girl in the road, and my wife called about her husband stuck in some kind of fucking bear trap. You—you need to get someone out here right away. Gina's disappeared, and you were supposed to be here hours ago and my foot really fucking hurts!"

"I'm sorry, sir, what did you say your name was?"

He gave it, and his phone number.

"Right, the guy with the dead bear. We sent an officer out to check on the animal. We didn't see any sign of foul play."

"What? No, no. I'd have seen the lights, heard the siren. I'm just off the road, and my foot is caught in a trap. You need to come back!"

"We can send another unit out, sir, but it's going to be a while. There's a three-alarm fire on Maple taking up most of our resources, and—"

"YOU SAID YOU WERE GOING TO SEND A FUCKING AMBULANCE!"

"I'm sorry, sir, if there was some miscommunication. We'll dispatch an ambulance right away. Just stay put."

"Okay. I'm in the woods just off the road. My car is parked on the shoulder." He gave the make and model, again, and told him he didn't want to stay on the line because his battery didn't have much left in it.

The line went dead. Eleven percent.

He shivered. Fog rose from the ground, pocketing in the low areas before spreading to envelop the low-lying vegetation. It swallowed sound.

Red lights flickered in the mist. He sat up on his elbows and cried out. "Hello? Hello!"

No one replied.

"I'm in here! I'm over here!"

He called 9-1-1. It rang and rang, but no one picked up.

"HELLO! I'M RIGHT OVER HERE! HELLO!" He screamed himself hoarse, eyes rolling back in pain as the effort shook his body and jiggled his foot, resulting in spasms lancing through his leg. But still he screamed, and screamed.

A few minutes later he heard a bang, what might have been a slamming door. The red lights faded and disappeared.

"No no no no no no no…" He tried to keep from hyperventilating, squeezed his eyes shut against the impossible nightmare his night had become. He'd planned on dropping Gina off at work, picking up a sixer of Labatt and watching whatever happened to be on cable. Now he lay in feverish panic, hoping his wife or the EMTs or somebody, anybody, would come and take away the deepening, soul-rending ache in his leg.

He cried, and he laughed, and he called out for Gina. If the trees listened they didn't reply, and the moon continued its march toward the horizon, now just a lighter patch of blur behind the fog that whirled between the branches high above.

Rustling brought his hysterical breathing to a hitching stop. He held his breath as it got closer, and closer.

"Jim?"

It exploded from his lungs in a rush, and he sucked in another.

"Oh, my God, baby, where have you been?"

Gina shuffled up next to him. She cradled the little girl against her chest, still covered in brown-red gore. It dripped onto his face, hot and wet, slippery. He jerked his head away as she kneeled down.

The girl's head wobbled back and forth on her breast, like an infant feeding. Gina smiled down at him, her eyes a glassy silver. She didn't blink.

"I found her, baby. Or she found me. And she needs us."

He tried to reach up, tried to push her away, but couldn't find the strength.

"She's been out here so long, and so lonely and hungry." She set the girl on the ground next to him, and as she pulled away a strip of tit tore away with a wet sucking sound. Blood dribbled from the girl's lips in a long trickle to spatter the leaves next to his head. The wound gushed, a fist-sized hole where Gina's nipple had been.

The girl nuzzled into his neck. He squirmed, tried to pull away, and Gina's fist pounded down on his trapped foot.

He screamed at the overwhelming, unending hurt of it, and screamed again at the tiny, dagger-like pricks that tore at his jugular. A hot wash of liquid spurted from the wound, and his vision faded. The mist shimmered, turned to silver in his eyes, and in it a thousand faces screamed with him.

The Getaway

by Patrick Freivald

The silver BMW sedan screeched to a halt as Bud bolted in front of it, 12-gauge raised and pointed at the windshield. His hands shook, and acrid wisps of gunpowder still rose from the barrels.

"GET OUT OF THE FUCKING CAR!" The high squeak in his voice couldn't drown out the wailing alarm or the screaming from inside the jewelry store, but the driver had to have heard him. Hands at ten and two, the old man's bright green eyes stared at him as the only points of color in a wrinkled, liver-spotted head. His blank face betrayed no emotion, and his pupils didn't so much as flash.

"NOW!"

The locks popped up, and as the man fumbled with his seatbelt Bud yanked the door open. Tangling fingers in his maroon cardigan, Bud jerked him out of the car and into the other lane, where he sprawled to his hands and knees, then fell to his side. Getting in, he hit the button again to unlock the back doors.

Alan piled in, dragging Jimmy up and inside.

Bud floored it, and the back door closed and bounced open again, eliciting a groan from their best friend.

"How is he?" he asked, shifting from third to fourth, the motor rumbling a Tiger's purr as they shot down the street toward the desert.

With a grunting heave Alan hauled Jimmy's legs in, and the wind slammed the cabin closed.

"Hospital," Jimmy muttered.

"No!" Alan held up a hand, soaked red-black with Jimmy's blood. "He's going to die. No reason we need to go to jail."

Bud sneered, half desperate grief, half desperation. "We can't just—"

"Fuck him, Buddy. This fucking job was his goddamned idea. And you shot a guard, man. We'll get the chair." Alan pulled Bud's ski mask from his face and smeared his hand down his cheek, wet and warm and sticky.

Bud turned his head away, but had nowhere to escape to.

"It was self-defense." The words turned to ashes as they left Bud's mouth. He didn't believe them any more than a Maricopa County jury would. Yeah, the guard had shot first, but they'd busted in with weapons up.

Alan looked down as Jimmy coughed, stroked his hair. "Nice plan, dickhead."

Bud and Alan had wanted to rob the place during Jimmy's shift, split the goods later after making a good show. Jimmy had pussied out, said Walters wouldn't put up a fight if they hit it on his shift. Well, the dumb fuck had shot Jimmy before he'd finished yelling "HANDS UP!" and Bud did what he'd had to do.

He licked his lips and took a hard right, toward the emergency clinic on Manzanita Drive. "We need to—"

Something thumped in the back of the car.

"The fuck was that?" Alan's eyes bugged in the rearview mirror.

"I hit something."

It came again, and again, a series of knocks from inside the trunk. While Alan wigged, Bud floored it. The knocking continued until Alan wailed, an eruption of sorrow. He babbled, most of it some combination of "wake up" and Jimmy's name, before looking up into the mirror, red-eyed and deflated.

"He's gone, man."

Jimmy's bowels let go in a burst of flatulence, and the car filled with the stench of piss and shit.

"Ah, fuck me," Alan said. "Pull over. Pull over!"

Bud hit the brakes and slid onto the dirt shoulder, kicking up clouds of dust. He got out and helped Alan with Jimmy's body, his black shirt soaked through, lips pale and white beneath his mask. They dropped him on the shoulder, and Alan tore off his own mask, revealing a thin, ruggedly tan face with a blond pencil mustache and eyebrows to match.

Bud looked down at the body, and his gut twisted. "What do we do?"

The trunk shuddered with another bang.

They exchanged glances, then Bud fumbled with the keys, dropped them. Alan picked them up, hit the "Trunk Open" button on the fob, and stepped back with one hand on his revolver.

It flew open and a pair of dark brown legs popped out, thin and muscular and slicked with blood.

"Holy fuck!" Bud rushed forward.

The squirming red thing in the trunk blended too well with the slick plastic encasing it, thrashing and sliding around too fast for his eyes to resolve. It froze, and he gasped.

She stared at him with wide eyes, pale blue against bloodshot white. A filthy rag held a soaking-wet glob of fabric in her mouth, tied so tight she couldn't close her jaw. Thick plastic zip ties, like the ones cops use, held her ankles together, and another pair criss-crossed her wrists behind her back. A ragged, scabby hole remained where her left ear should have been, and her bottom lip had been cut away to reveal square white teeth. Gouges and burn marks scarred her body, and several fingers on each hand bent at unnatural angles.

"Fuck me." He reached in, slid his arms under the plastic bag that mostly encased her body, and lifted her out of the trunk. She screamed through the gag, a muffled cacophony of panic and pain, and her head wrenched around in violent shakes.

He held her as Alan grabbed her hair in a rough fist and sliced through her gag, his knife running smoothly up the back of her head, blade outward. Two more cuts and her wrists and legs were free.

She pushed the wad from her mouth, revealing a tongue spotted with white burns and several missing upper teeth. "Nononononono..."

He comforted her while she babbled, stroked her hair, and bugged his eyes out at Alan, who put away his knife to search the trunk.

"It's okay," Bud said. "We're going to get you out of here."

Her babble escalated into a wail that resolved into garbled, misformed words. "NO! No! You can't! You have to give me back! If you don't give me back he'll—oh, God. Please! You can't take what's his and get away with it. You have to give me back!"

"Shhh... He can't hurt you now. We'll get you to a hospi—"

Stars exploded across his vision as her forehead crushed his nose. Stumbling, he let her go, and his breath left him in an explosion of agony when her knee contacted his balls.

Gritting his teeth, he stared in appalled fascination as she shoulder-blocked Alan out of the way, stuffed the bag back into the trunk, and started to climb in. Her screeching might have been, "Take me back!"

Both the noise and her frantic movements stopped when Alan struck her in the temple with the butt of his pistol. She collapsed in a heap, half-in and half-out of the compartment. He grabbed her by the armpits, dragged her to the shoulder, and dumped her next to Jimmy.

Bud looked from the bodies to Alan and back. "What do we do?"

"I'm getting the fuck out of here." Alan walked around the car to the driver's side. "If you're coming, get in."

He got in. Three hundred miles and half a pack of cigarettes later they stopped for gas at a run-down shithole with two sets of pumps and a tiny store attached, the last stop before a long stretch of desert between there and Vegas. Bud had cleaned as much of the blood as he could from his face and neck, and the rest didn't show up well on their dark clothes. The radio hit on the robbery at every commercial break, but with no description of the suspects beyond "white males," and no mention of the car or the old man.

Bud went inside to buy supplies—more cigs, sandwiches, beer—while Alan pumped gas. He made it three steps before the bell jingled behind him and a rough hand grabbed his arm. Turning, he met Alan's wide eyes, looked down to see the bag of money and jewels in his hand.

"Dude. We got to go."

"I just—"

Alan yanked him toward the exit. "NOW!"

They walked out, and Alan pulled him away toward a rusty minivan, and the young pregnant woman filling it with gas. Bud's heart hammered, and he looked around for the police.

"Lady," Alan said. "You local?"

"Uhhh," she looked back and forth between them. "What?"

"Are. You. Local?"

"I don't know—"

"Do you live around here or are you just passing through?"

"Oh." She stepped back as he didn't quite invade her personal space. "I, uh, I live a couple miles down the road."

"Good. How much for your ride?"

"Excuse me?"

He reached into the bag, pulled out a wad of bills and gold, and shoved it at her chest. Her hands closed over it, and her brow furled. "That's like, eight grand."

"Wait, what?"

Taking Alan's cue, Bud got in the passenger's side and checked it for problems. Two car seats, piles of trash on every surface—mostly fast food containers but also shreds of diaper boxes and opened packets of powdered formula—but no kids. Outside, Alan shoved another handful into her hands, tore the spigot out of the van, and snatched the key from her outstretched hand.

She smiled as they pulled away. Bud waited until the station had faded into the distance before speaking.

"Cops? You know they'll use that shit to find us."

Alan shook his head. "Not cops. When I opened the tank I found this." He held up the crushed remains of an electronic device, black plastic and a couple LEDs with an open compartment for a button battery.

"What the hell is that?"

"Tracker."

"How do you know it's a tracker?"

"It's a fucking tracker. Psycho dude keeps a girl in his trunk and has some blinky widget hidden in his gas tank? It's a fucking tracker." He put his hand out the window and let it fall.

"So he knows we're headed to Vegas."

"Not anymore. I'm going to cut back to 40 to California and head for Tijuana. Fuck this whole fucking thing, I'm out. You want to bail you can bail, but I keep the van as part of my share."

"Yeah, no, man. Tijuana sounds good. Who the fuck is this dude?"

"I don't want to know."

Two hours later they raced the sunset south of the Mojave National Preserve, and pulled into a motel conveniently located next to a three-aisle liquor store with a backlit red and white sign that said only "LIQUOR", and a gazillion square miles of nothing. Alan hummed "Hotel California" as they checked in. The grizzled cowboy at the desk took cash without questions and made change for the laundry machines without more than a glance away from the basketball game on the giant flat-screen TV that might have been the only part of the place newer than 1975.

They parked around back, hidden from the road, bought a bottle of Jim Beam from the Native American dude at the apparently-nameless liquor store, and settled in.

Bud chugged as he slipped off his shoes, savoring the harsh burn in his throat and the spreading warmth in his gut before passing it off to Alan. His hands shook as he unbuttoned his pants. "I'd fucking kill someone for a joint right now."

"Amen to that." Alan hefted the bottle, drank a third of it, and set it on the table between the beds without putting on the cap. "This is fucked, man. So, so fucked. He cut off her lip. Her fucking lip."

"Did that girl really get back in the trunk?"

By way of reply Alan swept up the bottle and held it out.

Bud took another three swallows, not as warm but better tasting than the ones previous, and his stomach lurched. "I'm starving. And I need a shower."

Alan fell back on his bed, fully clothed, arms outstretched. "Food tomorrow. Tonight we pass the fuck out, then get the hell out of Dodge first thing."

Bud nodded by way of agreement, stumbled into the bathroom, and didn't look at the scruffy, bedraggled, broken-nosed murderer in the mirror. The guilt in that man's eyes might kill him, as dead as Jimmy, as dead as Walters. The white porcelain sink, long ago stained yellow with rust, didn't tell him whether or not Walters had a family, a girlfriend, people who loved him. He had to. Bud stripped, turned the shower on as hot as it would go, and got in.

The heat and hunger and booze scoured his tears, washed away blood as he sobbed against the wall. He cried for his friend, his victim, the crazy tortured girl. But mostly he cried for himself, and he cried all the harder for being such a selfish piece of shit. He'd killed a man, and wept for his own tears.

After a while—twenty minutes, maybe forty—the water turned lukewarm. He turned it off, dried on the scratchy blue towel from the rack above the sink then wrapped it around his waist.

"Hey, Alan," he stepped around the corner, using the doorframe to support his vertigo-addled body. "Your—"

"Don't scream." Garbled words from a ruined mouth. The girl stood next to Alan's bed, Bud's shotgun raised to point at his knees. "Do something stupid we take your legs." By her side the old man looked at him with the same dead stare Bud had seen when jacking his car.

Alan still lay on the bed, arms and legs spread wide, a hypodermic needle empty next to the trickle of blood where his left ear should have been. Eyelids removed, he gaped at the ceiling, mouth working like a fish pulled from the water. Topless, a red ruin smothered the remains of his torso, where ropy blue-pink intestines spilled out across the comforter to pile intact on the floor by his feet. A purple bruise across his neck revealed where someone or something had crushed his voice-box.

Bud put up his hands. "Look, I'm sorry, man. I didn't know—"

"I told you," she said. "I told you. I told you to bring me back. I told you the doctor would find you and punish you."

He opened the door with a liver-spotted hand and gestured outside, then stepped through without waiting.

Bud swallowed. "Where are we going?"

"Outside," she said.

He shuffled to the door. She followed, ten feet back—way too far to make a go for the gun.

The BMW sat idle in front of the door, open trunk lined with fresh plastic. The pregnant woman from the gas station lay inside, hogtied with zip ties. Eyes wide, her muffled screams shrill and hoarse even through her gag.

"Get in."

"No." He shook his head, stepped back. "I'm not getting in there."

A ragged gurgle sounded from her throat, and it took him a moment to recognize a chuckle. "Your friend, there. It's going to take him hours to die. Hours and hours, and he'll be awake the whole time. No shock, no respite. You want to be like him, or like me?"

He turned. She stepped back, eyes flat, finger on the trigger.

"Please. Why are you doing this?"

A half-shrug slipped her white shirt down her shoulder, revealing a fresh brand, blackened red across her shoulder. "He wants me to."

"But I—"

"Get in, or we take your legs and put you with your friend."

"I won't." He turned back to the trunk, to the third person he'd get killed in two days, her tear-soaked face, the promise of new life swelling in her belly. A spark of resolve, the memory of bravery long withered, flickered in his breast. "Not ... not unless you let her go."

"All right."

He spun, with almost a smile. "Really?"

A sharp prick stabbed into his neck. He slapped at it, whirled with a haymaker made clumsy by alcohol and fatigue. The doctor stepped back, and he missed by a mile.

The earth shifted as her shoulder-block took him back two steps until his knees hit the bumper. Flailing, he fell and his face bounced off metal. It hurt, but not like it should, more a dull ache, like a tooth after not enough Novocain. His body defied his will to fight, and instead sagged awkwardly halfway into the trunk. His arms wouldn't lift, wouldn't struggle, as the old man slipped zip-ties around them and cinched them tight. Then his ankles. The constriction felt far away, the distant nag of a cigarette jones twenty minutes after you'd gone to bed.

"You can't do this." He meant to say it, but the words came out a low moan.

He felt himself shifted, floating, and a low rumble screamed through the gag next to him.

The doctor lifted both hands to put them on the trunk lid.

"Thank you," he said, his voice a dry rasp. His eyes flickered to the pregnant woman, still screaming through her gag. "For her. This will be special."

The trunk closed, and the world plunged into darkness.

About the Author

Patrick Freivald is an author, high school teacher (physics, robotics, American Sign Language), and beekeeper. He lives in Western New York with his beautiful wife, two birds, three dogs, too many cats, and several million stinging insects. A member of the HWA and ITW, he's always had a soft spot for slavering monsters of all kinds.

He is the author of *Twice Shy*, Bram Stoker Award®-nominated *Special Dead*, *Blood List* (with his twin brother Phil), the Matt Rowley novels including Bram Stoker Award®-nominated *Jade Sky* and *Black Tide* as well as *Jade Gods*, a growing legion of short stories, and the *Jade Sky* graphic novella (with Joe McKinney) in *Dark Discoveries* magazine. There will be more.

Pint Bottle Press
99¢
DOUBLE-BARREL HORROR
SHELLFISH
EXILE
KAREN RUNGE

143

Shellfish

by Karen Runge

"Sunscapes, seascapes, fresh salt air.
And even when we leave this place
Our memories will stay here."

He sang this song over and over again on our drive to the coast. First in an enthusiastic brawl that made me giggle–his big hands gripping the steering wheel, head tilted back, all white teeth and wide smile. A beautiful smile: a real one. Dimples pressed into thick, stubbled cheeks.

"Sunscapes, seascapes, fresh salt—"

His voice blasting against my ear, close and wild and a little too loud in the tight space.

Me telling me: *Just go with it. Then you'll enjoy it. Just go with it. Please.*

It was an eight-hour drive, and by the time we reached the halfway mark he'd dropped the rhyme down to a half-worded hum. When he fell silent for a while I'd catch myself anticipating it: those seesaw sentences, that raw voice. A voice too harsh, too masculine maybe, for such a childish song? Hairy knuckles gripping the wheel. Nicotine-stained teeth chopping soft words.

I kept the tip of my tongue pressed hard against my own tight-shut teeth. Wondering now, *Was this really such a great idea?*

Telling myself, *Be patient, be sweet.*

A schoolteacher tone, quieting my inner hell-child.

Be patient, be sweet.

The adult commanding the self.

Behave.

Me pleading with myself.

Because we might be wrong … right? Because this might work out … right? And what a sweet man he really is. What a wonderful, gentle, kind—

Him, taking a hand off the wheel to tap the tune out on my closest knee.

Sunscapes, seascapes, fresh—

And he shot me another glance to see if it would make me giggle again. A glance I didn't meet, trying to absorb myself in the passing scenery instead. A bunch of beautiful nothing.

"So… did you sing that song as a kid or something?" I asked, forcing myself to take pity on him. "Or did you just make it up?" The effort to ask this in an easy tone was gargantuan.

"Made it up on the spot!" he said. "Just for you." Then a little more quietly, "Just for us."

The word 'us' a lead balloon, a smouldering photograph, a sinister order that sounded a lot like *Love me.*

Or, *Because you love me.*

Or, *Because you're supposed to love me.*

How was I meant to feel now? Impressed? Moved?

My stomach hardened, dropped. Layering itself with lead. There was a fly trapped in my skull–this constant buzzing.

I forced a smile. "That's nice."

That's nice. Dear god, reduced to that polite, near-meaningless little phrase. Recalling a poster an English teacher kept on the wall at the back of the classroom when I was a child. THERE ARE NICER WORDS TO USE THAN NICE! screaming from the centre, an explosion of alternative adjectives cloudbursting around it, scrambling for space.

Except this time, the word 'nice' seemed about as dead-on as it could ever be. Because this *was* nice, really. *Nice.* Nothing greater, nothing lesser. As insipid as it was true.

"When were you last at the coast?" he asked me, and I forced myself to relax.

It's a decent question. Opening a fair conversation. Even if it is a question he already knows the answer to....

"Not since I was eight," I said. "Not in a very long time."

"Ten years, you mean?" he said, winking.

Dear god, flirting now?

But he's supposed to flirt with you. He's allowed to. He's your—you're his—

At least this was a little closer to the script that began between us a few short months ago. When flirting was welcome, when our briefest exchanges carried the giddy elation of a thousand possible alternative meanings.

Back when I was thinking, *This could be something.*

Reading the same thought in his eyes.

Now trapped beside him in his car, that churning in my stomach thickened to mixed cement, I made myself free a hand from its hideaway between my knees, and placed it over the top of his.

There. See? I'm trying. See? I'm being nice.

Because when I agreed to go on this holiday with him, I promised myself that I would try, at least. And try to be *nice.*

***

What brought us here?

An only slightly awkward evening a few weeks back. Drinking wine on my sunset-lit balcony. Eating skinny sweet potato fritters I'd made myself, crisp and oily, seasoned with coarse salt and black pepper. Evidence that a part of me at least was still eager to impress him. Me half-drunk with my bare feet resting on his knees, waxing lyrical about a seaside holiday I'd been on as a kid. The seashell necklace my mother helped me make, even now hanging off my bathroom door handle. Ornamental memories. I told him how my hair bleached blonde over that summer, how my skin bronzed. Long happy days outside in the sun altering me, improving me. I told him, laughing and shaking my head, about how I'd convinced myself I was really a mermaid. How every time I ran into the waves, I really believed that there might—just maybe—be a transformation. That my legs would quake and clench together, flesh moulding into flesh, silver scales sprouting from my skin.

I told him how there actually *was* a transformation, of a sort. Because when the holiday was over and we returned home, my teachers and classmates barely recognised me–I looked so different, I felt so different. Pale and mouse-brown to blonde and bright-eyed in a few blissful weeks. Shy and quiet to quick and smiling.

I told him this. All of this. About how magical I'd felt.

"Do you remember where you stayed, exactly?" he asked. And there was a sudden keenness in his eyes.

"No," I said. "But I wish I did. I would love to go back someday."

Over the next few weeks, he returned to the question every time we met. Whereabouts along the coast, more or less, did I think we might've stayed. What did the hotel look like. How big was it. What landmarks I recalled.

Until one Friday evening he invited me out to dinner, and there at the table he produced a neatly organised folder filled with brochures and screenshot print-outs of hotels, resorts, guesthouses. Grinning so wide his dimples tunnelled through his cheeks.

"Is it this one? It *has* to be!"

I nearly choked on my wine.

Because there it was. A narrow, square three-storey. White walls and slate-grey roof. Flowerboxes at the windows. Wide wooden entrance doors swept open, welcoming the light.

That quaint little place. That gorgeous little hotel. It's edges, for years murky in my memory, suddenly cut and defined.

I clapped my hands over my mouth. I laughed. "You found it!"

"I was thinking we might spend a long weekend over there," he said. "I've got a few off days owed to me. Just say the word, and I'll book us in."

It gets tricky, here. Something in my gut clenched. Tears caught and burned in the edges of my eyes. And I didn't know why. I honestly didn't know why.

An argument sparked off in my mind.

Those are my *memories. Mine.*

Well, he wants to make his own memories there. With you.

But they're mine.

"Wow," I said, clearing my throat. "My god."

"You called?" he said, winking at me.

Cheesy, but I let it slide.

"You did all this research? Just for me?"

"You deserve nice things. You deserve to do nice things." He reached across the table for my hands. I let him take them. Squeeze. His thumbs moved over my knuckles.

I had an urge to grab my salad fork and stick it in his forearm. It was the first of those kinds of urges, with him, and it took me by surprise.

"Wow," I said again. "My god." And instantly regretted it. But he didn't repeat the joke.

"Happy?" he smiled.

"Yes," I said, nodding. Deciding against myself. "Happy."

And I drained my wineglass.

***

My euphoria was only half-forced when we arrived at the hotel. The drive had been long and more than a little maddening. Nails on chalkboard. That echoing screech. My back ached, my buttocks were numb. The start of a headache was pressing at my temples. Tom carried the bags and I lagged behind him for a few paces, letting the distance grow.

Alone, alone. A moment alone.

Breathing in balmy air and feeling the ocean breeze push at my back, thicken through my hair. This feeling–I'd forgotten this feeling. Something beautiful and unnameable talking to me in the cast of new light (so bright!), the rush of the waves, the seagulls with their white throats and neat-cut, tapered grey wings diving and circling above. I felt like a schoolgirl, nervous with excitement and desperate to burst into this space and notice everything, touch everything, experience it to all its heights.

Desperate to enjoy.

Catching a quick, ridiculous hope that Tom had booked us separate rooms, perhaps?

On a romantic weekend away? Don't be a fool.

But this isn't a romantic weekend! It's supposed to be for me! About me! For me and … my memories…

Tom turned to wink at me as he walked up the steps. Half-dimple grin.

No such luck.

***

The woman at the reception desk was old painted young, her hair dyed lacquer-black, heavy eyeliner arcing up toward her temples, Egyptian-style. She was also more than a little familiar. As I was a little familiar to her, too.

"Have you been to us before?" she said, squinting across at me with a half-smile on her pastel-pink painted lips.

"Once," I said, smiling. "Years ago. Back when I was a little girl. I doubt you'd remember…?"

"I've been here since the start," she said. Warm, not sharp. "And I never forget our guests' faces. What's your name, honey?"

"Teresa Oldfield."

"Oldfield… Teresa…"

"But everyone called me Tress. Still do."

"Tress," and her smile trembled for a moment, then widened. "Of course. I remember you very well! You ran all over the place like it was your personal playground. David just adored you."

"David?"

"That little boy you met while you were here. You spent every waking moment together. You don't remember?"

A boy? David?

I shook my head.

"I would think you should," she said. Not sharp, not warm. She watched my face.

The moment twisted on us, stiffened.

Tom found my hand. I squeezed back. Grateful.

"Where do we sign?" he said, laying his driver's license down on the desk.

***

A strange fact. In the three-plus months that Tom and I had been (dating? courting?) seeing each other, we only managed to have sex a bare handful of times. What should otherwise be known as the 'honeymoon phase' (never enough time alone; bodies crushed together; gasping through that thick, tornado tightness) had passed us by entirely. Waking beside him on the odd occasion that he stayed the night, his hand would slide over my hip, drift to my belly, down … and I felt not excitement, but dread.

That was it. I dreaded him.

Strange, strangled-carrot shaped penis that curved down instead of up, denying my cervix that gorgeous pressure slide. Foreskin-stink that had me tearing at condom wrappers with my teeth–easily misinterpreted by him as my eagerness to get started, of course. And every time, he pushed me down onto my back without request. Missionary: the go-to move of the unimaginative. And then his gut swamping me, sticking to me so that I could barely move my hips, let alone tilt my pelvis to maximise my own chance of pleasure. And the sweat. Pouring off him within a few measly minutes of effort, splashing down onto my face and chest in drops of cold shock.

Water torture. You could call it that. The size and weight of him turning a man into a trap, making it impossible for me to squirm out the way.

Arousal. Excitement. Gone from me. Confined now to my memories of better times with better men, vibrator in-hand. Simulating the sublime.

But he's a good man, and he's trying so hard, and you've let him come this far–you can't just throw him away–you can't—

My inner voice was hysterical when we opened the door to our suite, set our bags down, and I found myself facing the bed. A beautiful bed, antique four-poster with an exquisite white lace coverlet laid over the sheets. The room smelled both sweet and musty, like sherry and potpourri. It was toned by glossy dark wood and subtle floral wallpaper; everything about it delicate and detailed and neat. If I searched for it, the sense of a memory came to me. Running my hands over a coverlet just like this, a wall papered just like that.

My mother saying: *Don't get that dirty.* Not sharp, not warm.

My father's hand on my shoulder. My mother's voice, lifting towards laughter.

"Wowee," Tom said with a whistle. "Is this granny's house or what?"

I caught my tongue between my teeth. I counted to five. "It's … well, it's guesthouse style," I said. "Not one of those … you know, blank modern monstrosities. You don't like it?"

"You couldn't swing a cat in here," he said. "Not without breaking something, at least. And I don't mean the cat."

He laughed. I didn't.

He sat down on the edge of the bed, and reached out to me.

A giant baby. A giant, spoiled baby, arms up, wanting. There'll be a tantrum if you deny him. There'll be—

I made my mouth smile, but couldn't quite get myself to look him in the eyes. I stepped toward him and straddled his lap, my legs tucked neatly against his thighs. His arms closed around me.

He kissed my neck; slime-slide of his tongue. I opened my mouth to the salty warmth of his shoulder. Held my breath as I touched my tongue to his ear.

Bit.

"Naughty girl!" he said, half-flinching, almost laughing.

I climbed off his lap. "I feel filthy after that trip," I said. "I'm going to take a quick bath."

***

Water again. Warm and scented, not wild and salted. My bare body, buoyant, sacred. Kept secret behind a closed and locked door. A razorblade tracking my shins, knees, thighs. Smooth, soapy sweeps.

For who? For what?

For me.

Not the truth in its entirety, but good enough for now.

Bubbles stinging my eyes, creeping up my nostrils. I scrubbed my face. Harder. Ducking my head underwater, ears covered, wanting to stay there forever in that silence broken only by the muffled echoes of the hotel's inner bangs and ticks.

I climbed out with cuts around my ankles and bubbles up my nose. Sneezing, shivering, bending to clench the towel around those tiny wounds. Sweet swells of blood.

I was kicking myself for not bringing a change of clothes into the bathroom with me, but when I stepped back into our bedroom with a towel wrapped around me and a tight grin on my face, I saw that Tom had left.

He got tired of waiting for you. You took your sweet time, so he gave up on you.

Good.

You're supposed to feel bad.

Well I don't.

Relieved by the unexpected solitude, I unwrapped my towel, ran it through my hair, and went through my bag in an elated peace. Imagining it was my space alone, that Tom was nowhere near it. Imagining that I was free to bath for as long as I liked, to sleep and eat when the urge struck, to stay here or go out as my own whims led me.

What kind of mean bitch goes on holiday with her lover, and spends the whole time wishing he wasn't there?

The word 'lover' dropped over me in a damp, dark fall that left me repulsed, shivering. I got dressed as quickly as I could, wanting to be sheathed, covered. Protected. I left the room with wet hair and twisted bra straps, smearing on lipstick as I walked down the stairs.

There was no-one at the reception desk. The small square foyer was deserted.

And how was I supposed to feel now? Relieved? Disappointed?

I stepped out through those wide wooden doors and took a moment to greet the ocean. Endless blue with white-crested waves coating the shoreline in a smooth, sliding rhythm. Back and forth. Beautiful. The constant chaos sounds of the wind and waves combined into their own form of silence.

A place so loud has never been so peaceful.

A memory combed its way to the surface. The snatched-sense of one, anyway. A wild wind knotting through my hair, pushing at my bare legs. Me, shivering in my bathing suit. Then the feel of small curved fingers, pressing into my hand.

Go away, David.

That's what I said.

Those fingers, opening, closing around mine. Tight.

Come on David, stop it.

Ready to run across the street and down the narrow, wild path lined with dense underbrush that led to the water. Knowing he would follow me, not wanting him to trip me up. The way he crashed up behind me. Slow but agile—he could navigate the brush better than me. And he didn't know his strength. Were my elbows skinned, from falling? From tripping against him? I think they were. Knees, too. And the heels of my palms.

Don't be a pest, David!

Yes. I said that.

I was about to step off the pavement when I saw Tom's steady, solid silhouette coming back up the street.

"Hello, gorgeous!" he raised a hand to me. With the sun sliding down behind him, I couldn't see his face. Was he smiling? Grimacing? If I could look into his eyes, what would I see there? What would I want to see?

And what if it was hate you saw?

The thought hit me like shattering glass. Brutal, sudden. Sharp. He stepped into my space and I hugged him back hard and long, breathing him in, my eyes tight shut.

"Looks like the ocean has done you a world of good already," he said, half-laughing into my hair.

It was more than enough to break the spell. I pulled free of his arms. One step back.

***

Eating crabs at a tiny seafood restaurant two blocks away from the hotel. Sipping white wine, its slight effervescence stinging my tongue. Tea candles in tiny bowls of coloured glass, smoothing the light against the fading brilliance of sunset. Too many silent moments between Tom and me. Me, lacing the concoction before me with mayonnaise and Tabasco.

I forgot that I don't like crabmeat.

"I knew you'd love this place!" Tom said, shovelling a shelled prawn into his mouth, lemon butter lacing his chin.

I should've ordered what he ordered.

"Yeah," I said. "It's cute."

Cute. In high school, we said that word means *ugly but fuckable.* Why did I choose this word?

Because it is cute, forget the teen-wise definition.

The kind of quaint, back-road restaurant that travel guide reviewers would describe as *a secret gem.* Or more fancifully, *a hidden pearl.* The benches at the bar were made from long sections of varnished driftwood. The curtains had been roped to their rails to look like sea-seasoned ship sails.

Everything was both minimal and detailed, designed to a perfect balance.

"This food is incredible!"

Another shelled prawn, another squirt of lemon butter.

How is it that a grown man still talks with his mouth full? On a date, *no less?*

Except ... maybe this whole trip takes us out of 'date' territory. Maybe that was the point. It's this kind of excursion, between a man and a woman, that pulls them out of 'date' territory and into the 'steady relationship' zone. Meaning, maybe, you are now tied to this man. Maybe—

"I don't really remember much of this place. Not as much as I thought."

"Honey, this restaurant probably didn't exist when you stayed here back then. Or if it did, what's to say your parents even brought you here?"

"That's not what I mean. I mean… all of it. I remember it, but I don't. Does that make sense?"

There was a hand crushing its way into yours and you were looking at the ocean. The wind was blowing and your legs were cold.

"Well, you were only eight or something, right?"

"Yes. I was eight. I've told you that twice already."

For a fraction of a second, his jaw froze mid-chew. Then he smiled.

And what if he hates you?

"Okay." He swallowed, took a deep sip of wine, put his glass back down. "Well let's start with what you do remember."

"That's just it. You already know everything I remember. I told you all of it weeks ago. Now that I'm here, I'm not remembering anything new, not the way you'd expect to. Just getting these … senses."

"Senses?" Serious, eyebrow raised. It was this look I always liked about him. *This* look. Concentrated, interested.

Ready and able to solve the puzzle. Making me feel I could trust him with things. Making me feel I could trust.

"They're more sensory than memory. Like earlier, when we first walked into the room. I remembered touching the walls as a little girl, and my mother telling me not to get anything dirty."

"I'd say that's a memory."

"It is… I guess…" I put my fork down. "But I felt it more than recalled it. I heard her voice but I don't remember her speaking."

"Okay. Well. It was a long time ago."

My jaw clenched. "Not *that* long ago."

He laughed. "Alright, Tress. Have it both ways. Have your cake and eat it."

"What's that supposed to mean?"

He sighed, shook his head. "Nothing."

"No, what?" Sharp, not warm.

We're on the brink of a fight, here. We're on the brink of a break—

Because you've been such a bitch. Because you've been—

Tears hit the back of my eyes. Saltwater sting.

And what a shame. Such a waste. On our last night here, on such a gorgeous evening, at such a wonderful place—

Last night here?

First night. The first.

And maybe the last.

"God." I put my head in my hands.

"What's wrong, Tress? What's wrong?"

At my side so fast, kneeling by my chair, an arm around me. The smell of him so comforting. His body warm, close.

I tangled my way into his arms, my eyes pressed against the thick curve of his neck, feeling his hands slide up and down my back.

"Thank you, Tom. Thank you."

A miniature outburst of emotion, making a tiny scene in our quaint, ship-themed restaurant. I didn't care.

He kissed my shoulder, my cheek, my mouth. I kissed him back. Again and again.

***

You were standing on the beach and the wind was blowing. It blew too hard and the sand stung your legs like a billion miniature bees.

You grabbed hold of David's shoulder and angled yourself behind him, protecting yourself from the blasts of sand.

He said, 'Ouch.'

Did he say that?

Or was it you?

***

For a moment it was almost beautiful. Tom and I walking back to the hotel on slow, strolling steps. Our hands entwined, the cool evening wind fresh on our warm cheeks. Neither of us talking, neither of us in need of words.

Keep it like this, because this I can handle. Keep it like this. I like it this way.

As we approached we saw the hotel was lit up, and there were a few more cars parked outside. The sounds of music, voices, laughter, furled out from the ground-floor windows. Of course. The hotel bar doubled as a local watering hole. I wouldn't have known this as a child. I would've been upstairs in the room, bathed and kissed and tucked in, while my parents slunk down here for a nightcap. Social time. Adult time. With no little girl running hellion at their feet.

"I don't know about you, but I could use a drink," Tom said.

"Music to my ears."

We stood in the doorway, me just behind his arm, waiting for him to move.

"Where do you want to sit?" he asked. Self-conscious at the throng of strangers before us. Hesitant.

"Does it matter? Anywhere!"

Still, he stood. Making me lead. Making me be the man, pushing through the thin crowd towards the bar. Catching a splash of beer on my sleeve.

"Sorry Tress, you okay?"

"It's just a little beer."

Intolerable.

I turned away from him, leaning to catch the barman's eye. Then turning back to Tom.

"What are you having?"

He stood stuck, indecisive. It seems absurd, but at that point his insecurity was so thick I smelled it. A slow, rank undertone like stagnant pond water laced with bile.

What am I doing with this man? A man who can't even find us seats at a bar? Who has no idea what he wants, and no gumption to get it? Not even a drink. A fucking drink!

I sighed, turned back to the bar, and this time the barman came straight to me. Twenty-something-young with acne scars and a thin moustache. Something debonair about him, something sure, despite his youth, his spare facial hair.

"My lady?"

Smiling at me so I had to smile back. Tom frozen out behind me.

"Two top-shelf bourbons, double shots, lots of ice. Please." My smile even wider.

He moved with the swift confidence of a man who doesn't see much point in questioning himself.

"No," Tom said when I reached into my bag. "Let me get this."

"Fine."

Because that's the least you can do.

He gave the exact amount, no tip.

"Sorry," I said to the barman with my saddest smile. And slid an extra note his way.

"No problem, my lady. Thank you." He winked and turned away from us, money in hand.

"I didn't think to tip. Sorry."

"That's okay. Some people never do."

"Tip?"

"Think to."

The bourbon was strong and chill, ice cubes burning my upper lip.

"You've stopped looking at me again," Tom said to his feet.

I swirled my drink. "Have I?"

"You know you have. You've hardly looked at me once since we got in the car to come here. Since we arrived. Since…."

"I looked at you at the restaurant."

"You needed me then."

"Tom. Stop being such a victim."

"Tress. Stop being such a bitch."

And here we are.

"Hey!" The barman was back. "You don't talk to a woman like that in my bar." He levelled Tom with a look that would make a schoolboy duck behind his desk for shelter.

Tom's face flooded red with shame. I caught myself grinning.

"You know what," Tom drained his glass and slammed it back on the bar. His face was so fierce with outrage he was almost handsome. "I'm out." He pushed his way back towards the doors with the determined purpose I wish I'd seen earlier.

"Are you okay, Miss? You're shaking."

"I … I don't know. He … he and I…"

"Relax a minute. You don't have to go anywhere with him. Come on. Next one's on me."

***

The damsel in distress is supposed to fuck her saviour. It's in all the stories, coded into all the histories. It would be wrong of her not to.

A bathroom stall with a broken door latch. Panties hanging off one ankle, skirt hoisted up, top torn down. Plyboard wall, shuddering against the force.

This is more like it.

Fists banging on the door. "Hey, hurry up in there!" Laughing behind the threats.

Debonair barman and me, laughing right back. Me clinging to him for balance, arms tight around his neck. His hands in my hair. Turning his face from mine to say, "Just a minute!"

A minute? God I hope not.

But this is what it's about, really. Spontaneity and power, elation, euphoria. *Fun.* This is what holidays away are supposed to be for.

And so in doing this, I am not wrong.

***

If the reception weren't closed, I might've tried to get a different room. Bleary-eyed and slightly off kilter, dumping my bag out on the desk, digging for my ID, the cash.

No such hope.

Back in the room, Tom was sprawled out on the bed, the mattress slanted on his side by his punishing weight.

And what am I doing with a man like this anyway? One who can't even look after himself. One who cares so little about himself that he let himself go.

I'd seen pictures before of younger Tom, of course. Lean and broad-shouldered, shy-smiling into the flash. Now his hair was almost gone and his waist was three times as thick. Only the smile was still sometimes the same.

Mermaid me and my dreams. And I come back here twenty years later, ready to settle for this. This!

I kicked my shoes off and unpinned my hair, which had been unravelling itself all evening and didn't need much help.

Tom moaned, rolled over. The bed sobbed under his weight.

If he breaks this beautiful thing, he's paying for it. Not that the money would make up for the loss.

"You're back," he mumbled, waking.

"Evidently."

"Did you have fun?" Sharp not warm.

"I had the time of my life, thank you. Mr Barman was an absolute gentleman. Well, sort of." And I laughed.

He was silent for a moment, blinking up at the ceiling with a frozen-glass stare. He turned his head back into the pillow. "I hope your head really fucking hurts tomorrow," he said.

"And I hope you won't be here tomorrow."

He was about to say something else, but then his stomach let out a long, gurgling rip that was louder than either of our voices.

"Oh fuck," he said instead. And with a swift grace I never would've imagined in someone so large, he rolled off the bed and ran to the bathroom.

***

David got sick too, didn't he? Coughing, spluttering. His nose and mouth wet with thick mucus.

Is this a memory too, or am I making this one up?

***

Sometime after sunrise I raided the top cupboards for spare blankets and grabbed Tom's pillow off the bed. He'd been locked in the bathroom for hours, and I'd slept right through. It was the stench that woke me, curling up from under the closed door, seeping in by the keyhole. Poisoning my dreams. I passed the pillow and the blanket to him through the door and the moment that air hit me, I blasted the scent back out through my mouth and turned my face away.

Human waste, human bile, freshly unleashed. So much stronger than the sweeter smells of old wood, potpourri, sherry. The smell of the sea.

"Try to sleep in the bathtub, if you can sleep," I said.

"So much for being romantic," he said through the door. His tone like a mourning dog.

My head hurt, my stomach roiled. There was no saliva in my mouth—my tongue sliding against my palate like a thick strip of cardboard.

"It's okay," I said, surprising myself. My tongue knocked its way around my mouth like a hockey puck, when I talked. *Tap-tap-thwack.* "It could happen to anyone."

Silence. Then, "Thanks, Tress."

"That's alright. I'll bring you some dry toast a little later. You should try to eat something again at some stage."

Silence. Then, a clang as the toilet lid banged open. Tom's voice strangling itself up his throat as he heaved. *Choke-choke-splash.*

I felt sorry for him then. I did.

***

You wanted this place to yourself. You got it. So what now?

"I need a new room, just for me. Nothing fancy."

Reception lady had done her cat's eyes a little too thick this morning. She'd chosen peacock blue for her eyeshadow, smeared all the way up to her brows.

Giddy, a little euphoric (perhaps still a little drunk?) I licked my lips with my dry tongue and smiled at her. "You look something like Elizabeth Taylor, you know that?"

Her eyes froze on mine. "That's the idea." Sharp. Very sharp.

"Well, of course…"

She turned to her clunky old PC with its packing box-sized monitor, and clacked away with scarlet-painted nails. "We can do that," she said. "Trouble in paradise?"

"Isn't there always?" I laughed, or tried to. "Nothing too soap opera. Tom gave himself a good dose of food poisoning."

"Food poisoning? How bad?" Her eyebrow shot up. Glittered.

"He's locked in the bathroom. I've tried to make him as comfortable as I could."

"Does he need a doctor?"

"For basic food poisoning? I don't think so."

"You'd be surprised." She paused. "Well, he'll need some saline solution or something at least."

"I'll make sure he gets some salt."

She nodded. "The pharmacy is on the main strip in town, opposite the book store."

"Thanks," I said, though I hadn't really thought of actually looking for one.

"Here's your key. You're just two doors down from him. Not as much of a view, I'm afraid."

"That's fine, just fine."

"Will you be paying separately?"

I turned the key over in my hands for a moment. Smooth metal, cold. "No," I said. "No need. May as well put it on his card, too."

***

I wore a long dress, pale blue, with straps over my shoulders. Exactly the thing a mermaid would wear, if she wore dresses. I walked barefoot on the beach with the wind catching at the fabric, pressing it between my legs. Sand stung my ankles. My head throbbed, my eyes burned. I kept my sunglasses on to save them from the searing morning light.

This would be so wonderful if…

If…

This would be so wonderful if I were with someone better.

If I were alone.

If I weren't alone.

If…

If only I didn't…

If I didn't have…

If only I didn't have a hangover.

The beach was quiet so early in the morning, the air still fresh with the chill-bite of the darker hours.

I passed, or was passed by, lone joggers, lone wanderers, locals and their dogs. A few surfers whipped and whirled among the far breakers.

They are all just people, ordinary people. But I am more than that.

In my blue dress and my loose straps, my bare feet grainy with damp sand, I walked on. Taking slow, measured steps. The breeze pushed at my dress, fingering my hair into tangles.

I want to swim.

It's too cold.

I want to transform.

You will.

I was the kind of hungry that makes you feel sick. Nauseas and starved, my blood thick and slow as syrup in my veins. It was still at least an hour before any shops would be open.

The stretch of sand before me roughened, the rising rock beneath hardening my steps. Further on the rocks rose up in mammoth clusters, their surfaces smoothed by the tides, their edges jagged from the steady spray.

Like teeth. If you climbed up there and fell against a shelf, it would rip into you. Shred you. Just like teeth.

I stopped for a moment, closed my eyes, and stood in the stillness. Shivering.

David was here. David was here with me. Wasn't he?

I searched myself for an answer, but with that headache storming my thoughts it was hard to pin anything down.

Daring myself, I picked my way up through the rocks, stepping carefully from one flat foothold to the next, until I was standing at the top where the wind was harder and the view was wider and the ocean tumbled and crashed around me in a way that seemed suddenly monstrous.

Like it's trying to reach up and pull me down. Like it wants to pick me up and pound me against these rocks.

And what did Tom tell me once? *You shouldn't react to everything like it's the enemy.*

It had sounded like a criticism. I would've said as much, except saying anything like that would only have proved him right.

Was that when this thing started to crack, in your mind?

I don't fucking care.

Tom's sick. He needs your help. What did Ms. Taylor say? Saline water … and you said salt…

Fuck him. There's enough salt in the air. We're by the sea, aren't we?

I sank cautiously to my haunches, then sat on the rocks with my legs crossed over the shelf. The sun was bright and very warm, the air chill with wild sprays. Seawater sank into the fabric of my dress.

I'll stay here. Right here. I did it once before. Didn't I?

This time when the memory came it was clear and crystalline and vivid as an acid trip.

David and I played here. They said we shouldn't, but I said we should. David said the tide sweeps high, that if you're caught on the other side of these rocks when it comes in, there's no way to get back.

He said it, and I imagined my legs pressed together. Flesh melding, scales sprouting. I saw the tide rising and me swimming into it, far out to sea, then diving deep. Alone in the cold water. Gliding further and further down until the sunlight above was a bare luminous trickle, and there was nothing but black beneath.

Did I imagine that so clearly?

I did. I did.

David was wearing those little red speedos. I wore a seashell necklace around my neck.

"Let's go back to the dunes!" he said.

And I said, "No."

I said no because I knew he would do anything I said. I said no because I wanted to watch his face as I said it. I wanted to see what he would do.

"The tide will come in," he said.

"But we're both mermaids! We can swim!"

And I laughed. I remember that. Laughing as he frowned and stammered, and he couldn't stop me when I raced down the other side of the rocks, agile, determined. Delighted. Because he would follow me. I knew.

How powerful I felt.

Now years later, I sat on these same rocks and felt a queasy urgency churn in my gut. Needing something, not knowing what. I leaned on my elbows and put my head in my hands.

There were tears behind my eyes again. Burning, sharp with salt.

***

"Are you alright, Miss?"

The voice was male, wind-whipped. I opened bleary eyes suddenly sliced by sunlight, and saw a lean older man standing a few steps down from me.

"You've got to watch the tide on this stretch of the beach," he said. "You can get trapped. People have been swept out, before. Especially children."

I sat up, straightened. Not looking at him, I took him in. "I'm not a child," I said. "I won't die."

"I'm just saying, Miss. This isn't exactly the best place to take a *nap*."

The way he said the word *nap* was as infuriating as it was infantilising. I glared up at him, though the light was still too bright where he was standing, through that light that hurt my eyes.

"If kids are stupid enough to play around here at high tide," I said, "then they probably deserve to get swept out. Darwin Awards, you know. It should apply to children, too."

He stared at me for a moment, aghast.

"This isn't funny, Miss. These rocks are a tragedy waiting to happen. We lose at least three people a year at this spot. Tourists and children, every time."

"I'm not a tourist, I've been here before. And do I look like a child to you?"

I had the sudden, ludicrous urge to pull the straps down off my shoulders and show him my breasts. Instead I laughed.

"Alright, take it or leave it." And he turned away with a dismissive wave of the hand. I could tell from the way he stamped back down the rocks that I'd pissed him off.

"Good. Fuck you."

And in my head I heard Tom saying, *Tress. Stop being such a bitch.*

And I whispered back, "And fuck you too."

***

We were leaving in an hour. It was our last run on the beach, David and me, while my parents checked out and packed up the car. David wanted to play on the dunes one last time, and I wanted to climb the rocks.

He said "Don't, it's dangerous."

And I said, "We're mermaids, aren't we?"

I watched his face change. I knew he would follow me. But would he follow me back?

Later he was crying, snot and tears and wild water pounding against his back where he clung... clung onto sharp black rocks and I said....

I was somewhere higher up, looking down on him and I think I said... "Just swim..."

Is this real? Am I making this up?

I must be. I have to be. I must.

***

When I got back, Tom's room was clasped in silence, broken only by a steady *drip drip drip* coming from the bathroom. The smell within the walls had worsened. Sick and sweet in a way that sick things should never smell sweet.

Despite myself, I closed the door behind me and sat on the edge of the bed. It was soft and warm and if it weren't for the stink, I would've wanted to lie down right then and let myself sleep.

It would be nice to sleep through this. Sleep, and sleep forever.

"Tom?"

Drip-drip-drip.

"Tom, are you awake?"

When he still refused to answer I sighed, pulling my knees up against my chest. I listened.

He snores, you know.

God yes I know. Unfortunately, I know.

"Tom, are you awake?"

Are you a—

Unease reached a cold iron fist into my stomach, and clenched. A cold sweat burst from my pores. I jolted, as if to stand. A moment later, I did. I walked to the bathroom door, closed one hand on the handle, raised the other hand in a fist. And knocked.

Tap-tap-tap.

"Tom?"

I turned the handle, but the door was locked.

Only someone as weak and incompetent as Tom would get sick like this. Only someone as stupid as him would lock the fucking door *so that nobody could come in and check on him.*

The moment of concern switched over to intense irritation.

"Tom, for fuck's sake."

I knocked again, harder.

Rap-rap-rap.

Answered softly with *tap-tap-tap.*

Water running.

He can't even close a tap properly. Do I deserve this? Do I deserve—

A memory came to me then. A memory? A fragment, a vision, an image. Not here, not now, but both perhaps.

A boy in a rockpool, a man in a bathtub. Eyes rolled back to show not white, but grey. Shimmer-grey, mildew-grey, aquamarine and awful. Jaws locked agape, swollen tongues pressed tight against white teeth. Pressing so hard that those tongues filled their mouths and forced their way through to the fetid air. Eyes rolled up, tongues sticking out. An immature expression, even in death. A face boys pull at girls to make them giggle. Or scream. There was a stunning stillness to the arms and legs, limbs loose in neglected water, swaying not from their own will to move but from the will of the tide.

Tide? In a bathtub?

That tide. I made it when I opened the door (not locked, only jammed, needing a shove and not a push) and stepped inside, and looked down, and nudged a shock-white shoulder with a trembling, knuckled hand. And the thing in the bathtub, the thing I'd touched bobbed, its movement breaking the skin of bile and effluent that coated the surface of water around it.

Just as the boy stared back with his unseeing eyes, and when I nudged him he slid away from me. Away, to the far end of the rock-walled pool, where the waves would rise to snatch him far out for the fish to shred him and the shellfish to catch the last of him in fibrous tissue snaps. Even the most beautiful of shells collected on the shores was once a living thing that needed to feed.

A man in a bathtub. A boy in a rockpool.

Did I see this?

I saw this.

I did.

But it's okay. Mermaids can swim.

And suddenly I was smiling. I turned and leaned back against the bathroom door, my heart humming high in my chest. The bed was made, the room was only a moderate mess. And everything in it was Tom's. My own bag was neatly packed and zipped, waiting on the edge of my own bed in my own room. I didn't need anything from here. From him.

"Tom, I'm leaving now," I said. Warm. And sharp.

His car keys were on the stand by his side of the bed. I slid them off carefully, to avoid the sounds of them clinking together.

As I closed the door behind me, I thought I heard a groan. Faint, weak, fading. But it might've been an illusion. The sound of creaking hinges. Something. But then, what did I really care.

How magical I felt.

***

Heading back toward the highway in Tom's blue car, the evening sun was bright scarlet, bloodlit, the line of the ocean a sheet of black that sparkled in the rearview mirror.

The steering wheel was slick and Tom's third gear was a little fussy, but his car drove for me just fine. Surrendered itself to me just fine.

As the ocean finally dropped out of view and the salt slowly faded out the air, I caught myself humming something. A tune I'd heard somewhere before, sometime a long time ago, maybe.

"Sunscapes, seascapes, fresh salt air.
And even when we leave this place
Our memories will stay here."
Here.
Here.
Here.
Exactly, and only. Here.

Exile

by Karen Runge

Every morning, you wake at dawn. You wake hours before you need to, or want to, because there are lots of trees around here, and they're all filled with birds. Chatters and squawks splice through the sounds of the night crickets, rising with the sun into a shrieking cacophony. You thought you craved the sounds of nature: something different from the radio chatter you had to listen to every day back in that tiny, musty-smelling little office. Hyper-happy DJ voices, mindless jingles, repeated sound bites. Your keyboard clacking. Voices in your ear.

Day in, day out.

But now that you're here, the constant chattering of the birds tears you out of sleep at dawn. *Soothing.* You thought it would be. But there's nothing soothing about these new sounds, even if they are only birdcalls. They hit the centre of your ear like a bag of needles, imploding into the soft of your brain. You close the pillow over your head. You give up—slipping out of bed and into the cool, shifting shades of brightening dawn.

Day in, day out.

The evenings are no better. When the sun goes down, you sit outside on the back veranda and sip wine by candlelight. *Meditative.* You thought this would be. But this time it's the frogs down at the stream that bother you: croaking out their cracked-throat calls. Like rubber boots on waxed tile. Like tearing skin, amplified. Chinese bangles. Throat holds. Screaming with a broken neck. Or trying to.

You have this house all to yourself. The nearest neighbours are hills away, their lights twinkling across the distance at night like land-locked stars. You wanted it to be like this—far from the city, away from other people. In a house, and not the cramped apartment you left behind. Here, there are no more footsteps crashing up and down the stairwells, no more voices reaching in through the open windows. No more sounds of sneezing, fucking, pissing, leaking through the paper-thin walls. You wanted time to yourself. No more hours at your desk with earplugs muffling the city sounds to a low, somnolent hum. The traffic outside, from blare to throb. The radio in the office, from chatter to whisper. The phone ringing on your desk, from a scream to a squeak. No more people standing over you, either.

Your colleague and only friend: *"Elise? Elise, are you listening?"*

Your boss: *"Take those goddamn things out your ears!"*

You came here for calm, for quiet. But nature has its own chaos, and so does solitude. Now you miss the sounds of people; city life. Those strangers you didn't know or care about, who didn't know or care about you, living their lives alongside you in anonymous complacency. Even your friend. Even your boss. Instead of feeling calmed by the absence, you feel exiled. A child pulled from play and made to face the wall. A woman locked in a cell. Pacing.

You were so triumphant about this escape. On the day you left—in the very hour—you recalled a childhood memory of something you saw at a train station, back in a more innocent time. You were a little girl then, standing at a kiosk with your mother's hand closed around yours. Standing silent in the chaos of footsteps, voices, engines. People passing, back and forth. Through the crowd, you found yourself watching a woman who was about to board. She was haggard-faced and dark-haired, deep lines set in young skin. She put her bags down on the platform and took off her shoes, swiping them off her feet in swift, furious movements. She held them in the air and shook them, banged them together at the heels. Her face twisted into a sneer.

I shake the dust of this city from my shoes.

She climbed the steps up onto the train in her socks.

It was symbolic, of course. And you were only eight years old at the time, but you understood the gesture. You watched it, watched her, unsettled but smiling. That scene, recalled years later as you made your way through the airport, came back to you in brilliance.

Before you walked through the gate, you slipped your own shoes off. Tapped them at the heels. Boarded the plane barefoot.

***

You set up the old hi-fi. This is against the original plan—to let in sounds from the world outside. But you need the music to drown out the birds, the frogs. The hi-fi is clunky, archaic; technology from another time. You search the channels until voices crackle in through the dusty speakers. You turn the volume up loud, too loud. Telling yourself it's okay, because there are no neighbours to bang on the walls or knock on your door in their slippers. Tousled hair, accusing eyes, waiting on the other side. Still, you have to stop yourself from turning the volume back down. You bath with the door open so the sound can come in. Fuzzy music and static voices. You look down at your body, the contours of your shape warped by bubbles, soap scum, steam. You duck your head under the water. This isn't hiding. This is retreat.

I'm clean, you tell yourself. You shave your legs though there's nobody to touch them. Moisturise, tone, though there's nobody to appreciate this. This is what young girls do—groom themselves for themselves, taking pleasure in their unfolding beauty, dreaming of who they'll someday be. Is this what you're doing, too? But what are you dreaming of exactly? Or, who?

Standing in front of the wardrobe in your underwear, the thought crosses your mind that you could forget about clothes and spend the days naked. Who would care? Not you. Instead you choose loose skirts, roomy dresses, shirts with gaping necks that slip over your shoulders. You're dressing like you're fat, though the bathroom scales say nothing has changed. This heaviness you feel is not physical. It must come from someplace within.

***

The cupboards are packed with tins of soup, cans of fish, jars of pickles, boxes of long-life milk. There are stacks of dried pasta, packets of dried fruit. You planned this well, hoarding supplies so that it would be a long time before you had to return to civilisation. Make yourself visible, makeup and purse. Resurrect that other you. The one that smiles, presents herself, pretends.

Alongside the boxes of long-life milk, you have boxes of wine. Boxed wine! The travesty. The friends you've left behind would be horrified. But you don't speak to them anymore. You are out of touch; disconnected. In this self-imposed exile, there is no need to present yourself. Or to pretend.

You were worried that you might overeat, alone here with so little to do. Food is an easy distraction. Instead you sometimes forget to eat entirely, drifting through the house, the garden, nausea clawing at your belly for hours before you finally recognise it as extreme hunger. You boil pasta, pour jars of sauce over it, mix it with fish. Everything tastes either too bland or too metallic. Sodium stings the linings of your cheeks—there are ulcers in your mouth, they sprang up overnight. You struggle over each bite, throw the rest away, wincing at the screech of fork tines scratching at the plate.

A pint of milk lines the stomach.

Your mother taught you that. Milk is good. Smooth, nourishing, alkaline. It's not exactly eating, but it's something.

You open the cupboard, reach past the milk. Reach for the wine instead.

***

In the evenings, you move from the back veranda to the front. You tell yourself this is to get further away from the sounds of the frogs down at the stream—but the truth is you make the move to keep an eye on the dirt driveway that winds down between the trees, and on to the gate. But what are you watching for? Or, who?

You listen to the trucks grinding down the logging routes. They're far away, but the echo makes them sound much closer. The roads nearby are quieter. Sometimes in the evenings headlights swoop through the hills, vanish behind them, reappear. You track their progress. Your neighbours. Strangers. Living alongside you in anonymous complacency. If you made your way to their homes and knocked on their front doors, would they open for you, smile at you? Would they let you in?

I'm alone here because I want to be.

Or wanted.

I'm here because I chose this.

You did.

***

One of your closer friends gave you a vibrator before you left. That friend, with her sly smile and knowing eyes, handed it to you in a brown paper bag. Watched your face change when you looked inside. 'It's a talisman against loneliness,' she said, because she talks like that—throwing archaic poetry into the most banal exchanges. It sits now in your underwear drawer, because that's where women keep these things—isn't it? Sometimes you take it out and look at it, press the moulded tip to your mouth like you would a pen. Considering. It's made of smooth plastic, turgid rubber. Not hard, not soft. When you switch it on, it buzzes in your hands. A wasp sound, a hornet sound. Stinging, insectile.

You decide there's something unnatural about the idea of fucking a machine. You want warmth and power pushing into you, hands in your hair, breath in your ear. This object is cold, mindless. You lie back on the bed, stripped, and use the tips of your fingers instead. Flesh at least, even if it is just your own. Sometimes you do this as much as five times a day. Something to kill the boredom, tiny explosions to break up the hours—solitary, dizzying. You're looking for elation, maybe. But now your sexuality, always a friend before, seems to be turning on you. It's rabid, persistent, taking you by surprise. It attacks you when you're making coffee in the kitchen. When you're standing out on the lawn, looking up at the sky. But you don't fight it off. You follow it to a couch, an armchair, the bed. Surrendering to climax is easy. Opening your eyes again after is not. Blank ceiling, desolate rooms. No warm body to curl into; no light laughter or soft words. No heart beating against your ear, no fingers running through your hair. You stroke your own hair, twirl the ends, chew the tips. A childhood habit—this is a sign that you've regressed. Your clitoris, rubbed raw, throbs between your legs. The vibrator lies on the blanket beside you. Mindless, cold.

A talisman against loneliness.

Or a reminder of it, maybe.

***

You stop restricting the wine. No longer just two glasses per night, but sometimes three, then four. A bottle's worth. You listen to songs on the radio, softer this time, finding the volume you're comfortable with.

This is good for me, you say. And maybe it is, because you catch yourself laughing. Standing against the sky with the lights from the house behind you and blackness ahead, you dance—or almost dance, because it's hard to move with all that static working against the beats. Hiss, pulse, rush. Throb. Fading in and out. You sway to it, searching for sounds to follow, rolling your hips and lifting your arms. You tell yourself, *You don't need the music.* You tell yourself, *Just feel.*

And it gets a little easier.

You stop getting ready for bed at night—collapsing onto the mattress or across the couch in your oversized clothes, waking before dawn with your head throbbing from alcohol and your skin slick with night-sweat. Still, you sleep much better this way. Without the ceremony, the ritual: toothpaste and soap, moisturiser greasy on your skin. You are simply you. Your soul in this body, your body in this place. Now when you wake, you wake screaming—or is it laughing? Joining in the cacophony of birdcalls crashing in from outside. It feels better like this: matching the chaos instead of fighting it.

By now you're out of milk, so you drink your coffee black. You spend less time in the bath in the mornings, and more time standing naked in front of the mirror. Instead of gaining weight as you feared you might, it's falling off of you at a rapid rate. Your cheekbones are higher, hollowing out your eyes. Your hipbones slide under your skin when you shift your feet. They look a little like blades digging up from underneath. Sharp things encased inside of you. Pressing. Ready to break the skin.

***

Your friend—the one who gave you the vibrator—encouraged this getaway.

Go on! Take some time for yourself! Leave it all behind for a while!

You saw it in her eyes: the image she had of you, of how you would be in this time. Happy alone in the country house, rambling through the garden, reading books under the trees with a sunhat stippling light across your cheeks. She saw you dawdling along a country road, coming across some strapping young labourer from a nearby farm. He would be young—younger than you—a student with a holiday job maybe. You would sally up to him with your slipshod smile and your starved eyes. He would stare at you; stupefied. He wouldn't know what hit him. But this is not how reality works, of course. Your friend, a Harlequin addict, reads far too many romance novels. You've told her this, before.

Another thing she doesn't see: 'Getaway' does not mean holiday. It doesn't exactly mean 'retreat', either. What it really means is 'escape', with all the panic the word entails.

At your going-away party, she said, "I envy you."

But now you're not sure you don't envy her instead. Waking to her alarm each morning, rushing through her morning routine. Battling the commuters, taking her place at her desk. Swift and efficient at her computer with her fast fingers and her faster smile. You remind yourself that there's a lot of stress in that life, and isn't that why you left? This place is stress-free, or is supposed to be. But she at least is always *busy*. You would give anything to be busy again.

The radio turned off, the birdcalls throb through your head with the pulse of a headache. A migraine with no teeth. Pain: Even pain might be something to occupy your mind. From across the hills, you hear chainsaws buzzing. Moving blades. Screaming trees. Things that feel, at least.

***

You've been a fool. There's plenty to do. City sensibilities can do this to a person: make them forget how to look at the things that are less immediately demanding. No crisis, no rush. Country life is seldom about that. It's more about preparation, taking stock, maintaining things. The lawn, for instance. You asked for the groundskeeper to be sent away before you came because you didn't like the idea of some strange man walking by at random. But there's work to do around here, and it looks like you'll have to do it yourself. You can't walk across the lawn without blades of wild grass slicing at your shins. But there's also another, more serious concern: You might get tick-bite fever. People die from that. You would die from that. Stuck helpless in this house, paralysed with pain, losing your sanity to the hallucinations your dying brain painted on the walls. It's easily treated, but could you recognise the signs in time? You doubt it. Nightmares, headaches, the ringing in your ears—these are normal for you as it is, in this place.

If only I hadn't left the city….

But you're here now, you chose this. Your soul in this body. Your body in this place.

You dig out a pair of jeans. They're city jeans, sleek designer things that ride your hips. Not the best for outdoor work, but better than those ridiculous skirts, those linen pants, those awful clothes you chose for comfort which barely fit you now. You find an old vest at the back of one of the closets. It's white, stained. A *wife-beater*, some people call them. Man's clothing. It has a rip down one side, a space just large enough for you to stick your hand through and trace the edges of your ribs. If your city friends could see you now. You pull on a pair of boots. Rubber, black. They squeak on the floorboards as you head out the house.

***

You always thought gardening was more of a man's job; maybe that's why tackling it now makes you feel so assertive. The shed, certainly, is male space. Cramped and dark, lit by a bare bulb. There's a splintered worktable in the middle, scarred and stained. Its surface is covered with boxes of bolts, nails, racks of drawers filled with shining metal things you couldn't begin to name. The lawnmower is in the far corner, resting under a sheet of tarp. It's old, clunky; four wheels with a hubcap dome, the motor fixed on top, the handlebars caked with grime. It takes you a while to get it outside, longer to figure out how to start it—and once you do it bursts into action with a roar so loud you jump back from it as though it might bite. Laugh at yourself, your heart throbbing in your throat. You set to work, circling the cottage in gradually widening arcs, leaving neat paths of smooth devastation behind you. In the end you decide you like this machine. All that power, vibrating through your hands.

You could stop here, but when you're done with the lawn you find you like the work. There are thick clumps of wild grass growing along the flowerbeds and down the banks—sections the lawnmower was too unwieldy to cover. You stand under the sun with your hands on your hips and sweat leaking down your back, deliberating. You return the lawnmower to its place in the shed, cover it back over with the tarp, and survey the tools hanging on the far wall. Hedge clippers; garden shears; a large, heavy knife with a long blade. This last: a *panga*. You remember the name. The garden shears might be more appropriate, but you decide you prefer the knife. There's something intriguing about this object, with its wide flat shaft, its sharpened edge curved up into a shallow tip. Its impressive size. Riots and massacres have been lead with these things. Hordes of men drunk on bloodlust, charging into crowds. Swooping. Screaming. The only thing you'll be chopping is grass, but you understand the appeal here. Razing, as opposed to being razed.

You hold the curved edge of the blade to your mouth like you would a pen. Considering.

***

You're on your knees in the dirt with the late afternoon sunlight pressing down on you, your skin seared, your man's shirt wet with sweat. You keep your eyes on the blade. *Swing. Flash. Chop.* Through the grass in thick fistfuls, seeded heads tossed to the side once severed. Your left hand holds the grass at the ready, your right hand does the labour. There's rhythm in this work; beauty in its rhythm. You're crouched halfway down the bank, shoulders aching, thoughts drifting, thinking *I should've eaten something.*

Thinking, *Dizzy.*

Your muscles tremble under your skin. Your wrists feel brittle, like dried-out twigs. The grass bleeds green, sticky on the knife's handle.

Swing. Flash. Chop.

The ache in your shoulders builds. Monstrous. Probably you should stop, but you don't want to leave the job half done. You focus on the rhythm, the beauty of the flashing blade.

And it happens. The knife arcs, sweeping through the air. *Swing. Flash. Chops.* Into your hand. A spray of red shatters across the grass stalks. For a few brilliant, senseless seconds, you stare at this new composition — the handle in your right hand, the blade snug in the side of your left.

Cold, you think. *It feels cold.*

You take a breath, thick and deep. And when the pain hits, you scream.

The agony takes you out of yourself. You're a thing of action; no thought. You tighten your grip on the handle. You pull. The blade, embedded in the bone, stays fast. Your teeth, clenched, squeak against each other. *Pull.* You pull. You let go. Are you sobbing or just breathing really fast? Your cheeks are wet. Your breath stops. You tighten your grip on the handle again. *Pull.* There's a wet, sucking sound as the blade comes free—and your right hand flies back, sends the panga spinning. The knife lands somewhere behind you, flat on the freshly mown lawn.

You're on your knees in the dirt with the late afternoon sunlight pressing down on you, your thumb all but severed, your wrist running wet with blood.

Screaming again.

***

When you were a child, you had a set of cheap plastic toys called *Farmland Friends.* Cows and chickens and sheep and pigs, all small enough to fit in your hand, many with their eyes painted in the wrong places, even more with underbellies and legs misshapen by ridges of plastic where they'd leaked out of their moulds. The set also included fences and gates you could clip together in sections, arranging fields and corrals and pens on your bedroom floor. The carpet was red, not green, but you didn't mind that. Poppies, sorghum, molasses. They grow red, too. You didn't think about the floors of abattoirs—that other kind of pen. Surely red.

You played *Farmland Friends* for hours on lazy weekend afternoons, setting your animals up in your carefully ordered scarlet fields, without once thinking about blood.

The sections of fence all clipped together like they were supposed to, but sometimes there was a problem with the gates. Plastic pretending to be wood; weak, bending, stretched out of shape. The more you played with these pieces, the worse they got. Once you built a chicken coop, but when you tried to attach the gate, the notches in the plastic were too misshapen to slot in where they belonged. How could you keep your chickens if you couldn't shut the gate? The chickens would get away.

Fly the coop. That was the term.

You swapped the gate for a different one. It didn't work either. You switched the fences, the gate again. None of them would fit. Your happy game put on hold, you sat for what felt like hours wrestling with the tiny, pliant hooks—your shoulders tense, childish frustration building into rage.

It began to feel personal. Your toys were spiting you, disobeying you. You, little-girl-god, mistress of this miniature world. Defied. Sabotaged.

You picked up one of the small plastic gates. You put it in your mouth. And you bit. Twisting it until your teeth squeaked together and your jaw ached. Wanting to do it damage. Cutting the insides of your cheeks.

"What are you doing?" your mother said when she looked in on you, caught you.

"Punishing it," you said.

"Elise. It can't feel anything. All you're doing is breaking your toys."

You should've known you weren't cut out for city life. Or for the country, either.

***

Back in the house, you hold your hand under the kitchen tap. Water sluices into the wound, plays with the nerves, throbs in the bone. The pain is so fine, so delicate, so intense it's almost *sweet*. At least, this is the word that comes to you with your teeth clenched, that traitorous right hand of yours holding the left firmly in place. You want to take your hand away. You must not take it away. The water runs a thin, viscous red. The wound flaps under the flow like a winking eye. Its iris is hard and white.

You need disinfectant. You need stitches. You need gauze, and bandages, and painkillers. You need a calm, reassuring voice. There is you. Only you.

You turn off the tap and grab a tea towel, wrapping it around your hand in stiff loops. The cloth blooms red like dancing flowers. You watch the flowers expand, slow, stop.

Disinfectant. Alcohol? But you can't use wine on a wound. Can you? Or is there something else … turpentine? Bleach? Are they safe? You don't know. You wish you knew. You could burn the wound to cauterise it—use an iron or matches, or … did you see a welding torch in the shed? But that would deaden the flesh, do something more permanent. At the least, leave you with an enormous, unsightly scar. You think, but you don't know. You wish you knew.

Wasn't superglue invented in wartime, as a substitute for stitches? Surely there's glue of some kind around here. And duct tape, to hold it tight? You think. You think you know.

Cradling your hand against your chest, you head back out to the shed.

***

A few hours later, you're lying on the couch with your arm across your belly. Staring up, breathing fast. Blank ceiling, silent rooms. When the doorbell rings it takes you a minute to register the sound. Longer to recognise it. By the time you do, it's more insistent—interspersed with thumping sounds. Someone is banging on your door. For a moment you think, *Is the music too loud?* But there is no music. Only the sounds of nature, screaming at you from all sides.

You get to your feet. Gravity sends blood plummeting down into your injured hand. It throbs with vicious heat. You blink back the tears that sting your eyes and, one-handed, wrangle your jeans back up over your hips. Your underwear is twisted out of place underneath. You can't manage the jeans button, but you get the zip back up.

You open the door to a man. A stranger, of course. He's older than you, his hair streaked silver, his face lined and brown from years under the sun. He's handsome, in a way. You meet his eyes, your left hand hidden behind your back. He stares at you. Stupefied.

"Can I help you?" you say. As if there's anything you could possibly do.

"I'm your neighbour on the north side," he says. His eyes rove around you, taking in everything but your eyes. "We heard screams a short while ago, from this direction. Was it you?"

Screams. Screams coming from farmhouses. Screams carrying across country roads. How do they hear them over the birds, the frogs, the crickets? How do they distinguish?

"No," you smile. Should you be smiling at this question? Is that appropriate? *Present yourself. Pretend.* "It wasn't me."

"Are you sure? This is the nearest smallholding to us, and it sounded pretty close."

Your smile hardens. "No," you say, a little more firmly than necessary. "I think I'd know if I'd screamed."

He looks you over. Maybe he sees something in your face, because for a moment he's not just looking—he's analysing. And there's a glimmer of something more than concern there.

Horror? Fear?

He shoves his hands in his pockets, leans in. "You're not staying here alone, are you?" he says. "Or you've got a gun or something, at least? Robberies and home invasions aren't uncommon around here. You do know that." This last isn't a question. You mentally tack on the extension: *Or if not, that makes you a really ignorant bitch.* Because for a moment, you read the insult in his eyes.

"My husband will be back from town soon."

He nods, looks away. "Alright. I'll give you my number, just in case? You really should get on the radio too. Just check in every now and then. Everyone else around here does. Tell your husband."

Tell your husband. It may not be sexism exactly. It's more that he doesn't like the look of you. He doesn't trust that you'd take care of it. Regardless, it stings for a moment before you remind yourself: *I don't care.*

He scribbles his number on the back of a receipt, and his name. Johan. You glance at it, more out of habit than anything else. Careful with your movements, your left hand out of sight.

"Thank you," you say.

He nods to you. If anything, his smile is stiffer than yours. He turns and heads back down the veranda steps. You stand in the doorway and watch him go.

How very Harlequin.

But this isn't your own thought. This belongs to your friend.

***

You have to cut the wife-beater off your body. Kitchen scissors, steady right hand. It's just too painful, moving your left. Lifting both arms would be impossible—the slightest shift of that shoulder is enough to invite the pain in your hand up to violent, booming levels. You snip the vest at the shoulders and it slides to the floor, barely pausing on its way past your hips. Only then do you notice that there are sprays of blood decorating the grainy white. Looking down, you see some of the blood got on your jeans, too. This, then, is why your friendly-neighbour stranger-danger stared at you like that. On second thought, he should've done a lot more than just insist on giving you his number and lecture you about radio contact. Or maybe he's used to people walking around their houses covered in blood.

You drink wine now because you need it. Your left hand safe against your breasts, you lay a fresh box flat and wrangle it open with a paring knife. Not a panga. That cruel thing. You understand a bit better now why they're so commonly associated with third-world genocides. There's something sentient about them, something calculating. Brutal. The way they take control of the bearer, tricking beauty into the rhythm of their movements, adding force. Changing aim. Because you're sure now: It wasn't just the heat or the hunger or your generally confused state that sent your right hand swinging too high. It was the knife.

You sit on the couch dressed in nothing but your blood-stained jeans, your rubber boots. Your left hand is at home between your breasts; your right hand holds a drinking glass, half-drained of wine. You're tired. The pain, slowed from a roar to a steady hiss, holds you conscious.

The knife. That bastard.

You drain your glass, refill it. Again. And finally you fall into something like sleep.

***

You wake to the frogs screaming. Throat-holds, broken necks. Your hangover and your drunkenness have swilled together—dizziness and a strange, euphoric nausea thrum through you. Your nerves ache. Your hand throbs. The pain has nestled in deep, happy at home in its new place.

"You can't stay," you say out loud. The sound of your own voice startles you. And what were you talking to? Or, who?

I'm mad, you think. *That's it. I've lost my mind.*

And like any respectable insane person, the thought makes you laugh—loud and wild.

The air in the cottage is still, stale. You would like to open some windows, but they're old and heavy and you'd need both hands to slide them up. You stand and stumble into the hall. The front door, left wide open, frames a rectangle of trees in silhouette, solid black against a block of sky blooming stars.

The chickens, you think. *The chickens will fly the coop.*

But instead of shutting the door, you follow the promise of cool night air and walk outside, your left hand still raised, pressed against your bare chest. Your steps are unsteady, but you walk fairly straight. Across the veranda and down the stairs, and out into the garden. The scene of the crime. Your blood will have dried by now. Just a stain on the grass. Out on the freshly mown lawn, a silver mouth catches the light, smiles. A cold smile, a hard smile. You walk over to it. You pick it up.

There's surprisingly little blood on the blade—just a few rust-brown traces on the edge. Where it bit.

"You bit me," you say aloud, recognising this as truth. This time the sound of your own voice doesn't startle you. You sound clear, assertive. Sure. This is the tone you use when you're putting your foot down. It's the same tone you used when you said, *I'm leaving this place.* When you said, *I need to be alone for a while.* When you said, *I'm gone.*

It's the tone of voice you use when you're angry.

Because this is personal.

"You bastard," you say to the knife. This object has spited you, disobeyed you. You, mistress of the house. Defied. Sabotaged.

You press the blade to your mouth. You consider. You think, *The chickens will fly.* The edge slides between your teeth. *Cold.* And you bite.

This time the pain invigorates you. Like a battle: the deeper it cuts into you, the harder you bite back. You scream through clenched teeth—a scream of rage as much as of pain—and the blade slices across you tongue. Your blood tastes like tears, only saltier, thicker, stronger. It runs back down your throat and for a moment you almost choke. You rip the knife out your mouth and it slices through your cheeks on its way. A farewell kiss. The panga falls at your feet. You clap your hands over your mouth, and the blood rushes through your fingers, sliding down your forearms. *Warm.* The pain in your left hand rolls over, woken by the movement. It joins the crescendo in a thick, rushing roar.

You close your eyes on your tears. Your heartbeat pounds through your head. A migraine with no teeth. The knife leers up at you.

Sentient. Smiling.

Crickets scream.

***

You walk, though you don't know where you're going. Away. The buzzing in your head is high, furious.

Take those goddamn things out your ears.

There is nothing in your ears. You hear everything.

You make your way down the drive that winds through the trees and on to the gate. The gate, left wide open by safety-conscious Johan, reveals a section of dirt road. You've come this way before. But was it you? Or, who?

You lean your back against the fencepost, and use your right hand to take off your boots. They slide off easily, oversized as they were. One-handed, it's impossible to bang the heels together. You set them down, pick them up together. You raise them high and shake them. Then you drop them back to the ground.

Your smile breaks the clots that hold your cheeks shut. Blood leaks over your chin and down the sides of your neck. Warm, then cold.

You walk, the panga held tight in your right hand. There's something about carrying this thing, enemy or not, that makes you feel powerful. You see yourself charging into crowds, holding it high. Swooping. Screaming. Of course, it's this promise—and even if it is a lie, it's one you want to believe: *raze, and not be razed.*

Behind you, frogs croak their goodbyes. Twisting rubber, broken necks. The night air is fresh on your bare skin.

Maybe if you walk into dawn, some ways down the road you'll come across a strapping young labourer. He'll be younger than you, and beautiful. You'll sally up to him with your bloody knife and your slippery smile. You will present yourself. You will not pretend.

He'll stare at you. Stupefied.

About the Author

Karen Runge is an author and visual artist based in Johannesburg, South Africa. Her debut short story collection *Seven Sins* was published by Concord ePress in 2016. Her first novel *Seeing Double* is out now with Grey Matter Press. Visit Karen's blog at karenrunge.wordpress.com.

Coming soon from Pint Bottle Press!

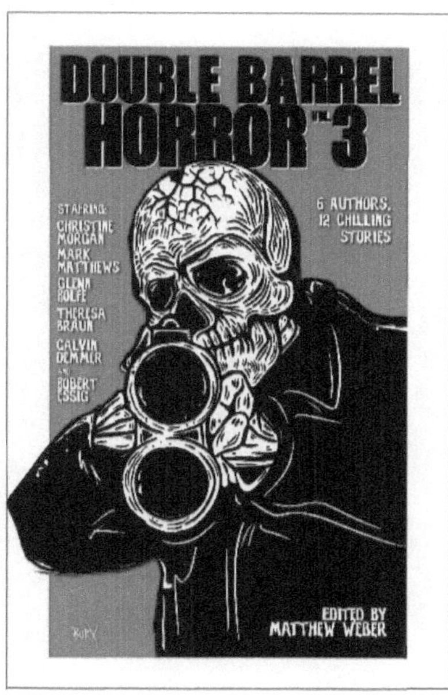

Available now!